Other Works by the Author:

the Everything Under novels
Sin Gorge
Jennyripper
The Never-Time Girl

"The World" Children's Novels
Beyond the Grass Ocean
The Nightly Train

Collections
Strange Symphonics: Short Stories for the Long World

the Virtuous (a tale of Pon-Chai the Thiefkiller)
Copyright © 2017 by Ron Horsley/Everything Under Press

Cover & Illustrations by Ron Horsley

ISBN-13: 978-0-9903910-1-2
ISBN-10: 0990391019

www.midnightersclub.com

Printed in U.S.A

the Virtuous

a tale of Pon-Chai the Thiefkiller

written & illustrated by Ron Horsley

Dedicated to my friend Lucy Snyder and my former teacher Tondaleigh Hall, who both introduced me to poetry that actually means something beyond catchy rhyme-schemes.

For Claire Wiedman, who has reminded me to stop and look at the walls and the trees.

And for Pretty, as everything always is.

"Leave the living to be raised...leave the dead to rise."
—Pon-Chai, 47th Dynasty Poet of the Caillou District
"Summer Unto Autumn In Gardenias"

Third Minister Adjunct-Willow smiled as Pon-Chai took the seat across from his. As if welcoming a private thiefkiller in a Gheru coffeehouse was an everyday thing for a lesser bureaucrat from the Franzhen court.

"Thank you for arriving promptly. And for respecting my request for no...tools of trade to be brought with you."

And wise that he had already reconnoitered the coffeehouse well in advance to be assured that he wouldn't need any. Only the lone attendant was serving, and the first floor tables were all empty. This was a private occasion.

The coffee set between them glittered and sparkled. Pon-Chai's eyes immediately took in that despite the shiny chrome finish, there were trace bits of tarnished silver plate here and there on the bottom of the sugar bowl, the surface of the pot facing him, a thumbprint-like smudge of the old metal on the handle of the cream carafe.

"Of course, had you attempted to do so anyway, this site has its advantages for such meetings." The minister waved a hand. Pon-Chai turned in his seat to look behind him.

The doorframe on this side of the threshold was carved, and the carvings inlaid with what looked like a filigree of silver and iron. Shapes that suggested clutching hands, upraised octagonal shields as in the First City murals of battles. Shapes that even as one stared at them seemed to become the gnashing teeth of creatures that disapproved of being stared at. He turned back to the minister.

"Repulsion glyphs," the minister said with a gloating tinge, as if he'd managed some clever prank. "Anyone who attempts to come into the room with anything approaching a weapon on their person, they are refused entry."

"A wise choice of meeting site indeed," the thiefkiller replied with neither praise nor derision.

"This establishment is one of my favorites. One can so rarely find a quality place in these lesser districts that not only makes an excellent brew," here he gently lifted his cup in salute, "but also has invested in some true security for its more distinguished patrons."

"Is Gheru district not one that you are managing?"

"I'm glad you received the summons promptly," Third Minister remarked, clippingly changing the subject as neatly as a spigot turning off the flow of water. He waved a hand to indicate an offer of coffee. Pon-Chai shook his head in the shallow twist-twist-twist of no-but-thank-you that was one of the court traditions in body language and greetings.

In response to the minister's comment, Pon-Chai reached a hand into one of his inner breast pockets and pulled free from his tunic the thrice-folded-over piece of square paper that was the dyed crimson of a fire at near-full-ebb in its embers. He placed it on a clear spot between the coffee pot and the cream carafe.

"I was told that was the proper form by which to send for you. I take it I was correct?"

Pon-Chai gave a respectful nod.

"For purposes of our conversation here..." Third Minister leaned back in his chair and made a small show of looking back and forth and slightly over his left shoulder in a suspicious gandernecking, "...do you have a preferred...discussion name I may use while we talk? The walls are old parrots, as you know."

"My father used to say 'the walls have ears.'"

"True. One saying as good and meaning the same as the other. But...?"

"You may call me Guest Ravensmall."

The Third Minister's quirked smile took that in. "Very well. Ravensmall, sir...I have a delicate issue that I believe only you and your talents can resolve."

Pon-Chai neither replied nor gave any indication to continue. He merely stared back at the Third Minister. It was a simple trick and the first that he'd learned under the Killer Master Three Brooms. It invited people you didn't want to hear from to shut up in fear of your unheard judgment, and people you wished to hear more from to open up out of fear of the silence.

The Third Minister leaned over his coffee cup, his voice going down to a hush.

"You are...just to establish our proper meanings and intentions here...a man who is skilled at...the wrangling of cuckoos?"

The bird that takes another's nest for his own. A low slang for thief in the Gheru district.

"Yes. I am practiced in such a profession. Have you lost a nest, then?"

Third Minister's mouth twitched down to a frog frown, giving him definite jowls of a middle-man.

"More like one of our most precious eggs."

This was less familiar conversational territory. Pon-Chai allowed an eyebrow to rise.

"You see...to put it as best I can for the stakes involved...I actually represent another party, who represent themselves another, smaller party. And lastly, all of us are...serving the needs of a singular party."

Royalty. He was referring clearly to royalty, Pon-Chai could almost visualize the tree of woven branches Third Minister described. The minister may be some lowly third-tier Willow branch, swaying with winds and keeping the waters of the pond clean of clutter in the bureaucratic worlds, but he was still of the government. And what regional government he served meant he worked for the greater Empire. And all the Empire served the Imperials.

"You are...not my direct client, then?"

"Better to not think in such terms," Third Minister sighed. "Better to consider me...your face client. Your payor. And who you will report to utterly in this matter." This last was delivered with a slight gravel added to the hush. And the minister gave Pon-Chai a face that no doubt he gave to younger servants to terrify them into giving prompter service to him in coffeehouses like this one.

But all Pon-Chai gave was: "I understand."

"So what we face here..." Third Minister looked down at his cooling cup of brew. Stirred a fresh spoon of sugar into it and stared at his spoon in his hand as he melted the sugar deftly into his drink. "...Hrm. What we face here is...someone has taken an egg that has yet to hatch, but is no less dear for its expected brood to emerge someday."

An unhatched egg. Pon-Chai frowned, then the metaphoric translation came to him like a low spark off a shock-bellied watersnake gripped loosely in the hands.

The Heir. The Heir Emperor, the inheritor of the rulership of all under the sky when he—or she—was born.

And if this minister was talking of the Heir Emperor, he had to mean the child that was even now known as four-months along in the belly of the First Empress Concubine. The child that would ascend to the throne over everything when it first breached its dame's legs and breathed air rather than mother's water.

"Someone has taken...the one egg of the great nest?"

Third Minister nodded and stopped stirring to look up at Pon-Chai studiously. "I think you take my meaning perfectly. And you can therefore imagine why so much...discretion. And care. Is called for."

"Yes." Someone who had managed, against all seeming possibility, to steal the intended virtuous name of the Heir Emperor? It could almost dizzy a grown man to really think hard on it.

With the virtuous name of the next Emperor Born, even the lowest Untaught could speak it and have power over the Heir. And power over the Heir meant effectively a new Emperor or Empress entirely...because anyone whose name was within the power of another was no ruler in themselves.

A single name for a child not yet even born could shift the world onto another pair of feet to bear it...and Pon-Chai was being hired to find and kill the thief who had made off with it before it got into the wrong hands...or more appropriately, *more* wrong hands.

"Do you have any idea how the cuckoo managed to make off with the egg?"

Third Minister nodded, and now made another gesture of stirring and staring with a dollop of cream and a cream spoon, almost dollhouse-fragile next to the larger sugar serving spoon or the regular coffee stirrers.

"It was three days ago—"

"*Three days?*" Pon-Chai was mystified as much as surprised. "Why so long to act?"

The minister gave a theatrical sniff and tightened his lower lip such that it bulged slightly from mouth.

"We are perfectly capable of handling many incidents of...the security of the nest...ourselves. Investigations were undertaken. Constables called and even *màgique* technicians consulted. Unfortunately whoever took the egg is very skilled indeed, as much in hiding away their escape as having taken the item to begin with." The cream spoon stopped. "It has taken three days to thoroughly vet the loss as genuine, and to ascertain that we were unable to secure it within our own...resources. Contracting an outside professional is not exactly our most favorite option to exercise," the minister sighed and flapped his hands gently like imitating a wounded bird, "but what can one do? Eventually we have to yield to our limitations and accept that there are specialists who have made such skills their bread and butter and so are in a better position to more expeditiously resolve things. I might add that it took the whole of the third day just for our assets and networks to locate you and send word for this meeting." The frog frown returned, this time looking a little as if Pon-Chai were at fault.

"Surely there are...official hawks, that may find this cuckoo at speed for you?" Yes. Armies, spies from the investigatory arm of the Screaming House, even some of the war adviser's own retinue of official *m'agique* wielders, the various Amber Teardrinkers and scriers who saw at great distances from the confines of a many-times-sub-cellar in a black room, only the light of their charmed marble basins to show them anyone in the kingdom they wished to find.

The minister gave a bitter smirk as he sipped. "Unfortunately, while there are many such hawks, there is...hmm...a finite space in which they have to spread their wings. And there are so many smaller birds amongst their roost...have you ever tried to find a single feather in a dovecote, my friend?"

Of course. So above any cautions the thief had taken, there was simply too much *m'agique* entrenched around the court. With all the protection wards, weather sigils, detection and surveillance spirits charm-trapped in various vital corners...of course any attempt to scry out someone within the very capital grounds must be met with the equivalent of trying to single out a single gull's cry at high tide.

"My information told me that you are considered a successful...hawk... owing in particular that you do not hunt as the others do. You prefer your own wing to riding the unseen drafts?"

"Yes. I do not use those...extraordinary methods. I rely on only my own wing and eye and beak, nothing more miraculous."

"A miracle is very nearly what I have in mind in employing you to enact for us, good sir."

Pon-Chai noticed the crimson paper still sitting on the tabletop in front of him. He collected it and returned it slowly to his tunic's inner pocket, using the slowness of the motion to give himself pause for thought.

A Royal commission...not officially of course. Like most clients for his services, nobody wanted it to be public knowledge that a virtuous name of someone in power or high privilege was loose. It would only be tossing chum into shark pools and then stupidly expecting every tailfin to politely ignore and wade away from the spreading scent.

"If I undertake to recover the egg...there are conditions under which I must operate. These are not unique to your need. They are the rules by which every recovery is achieved."

"Of course. I would expect nothing else."

"The first condition is quite universal and all-encompassing: I am the sole contractor of this task. No overseers or oversight. I report to you, but I will be the only one to report to you. This is not a *team* effort, as it were."

"Understood. And for the sake of our...other parties...we would prefer it just be you as it stands."

"The second condition is also that half my payment is before the mission, the second half is to be paid upon its successful completion. The first half goes to help cover my costs in the task. Any remainder of that half is forfeit upon my failure." No need to really elaborate—especially in these secretive chambers—that failure would likely mean his death and then what did he care for quarters, halves or any fees or anything ever again?

"Already expected and merely awaiting my making a few brief notices to my superiors and it will be in trust at your specified arbiter's house in your designated pay-name."

"That is acceptable."

The minister held up an index finger. "I must ask a condition of you in this while we are thus making arrangements."

"Go on."

The hand and its finger lowered to the table. The minister leaned forward, his wagging chin over the coffee pot now, almost fully risen from his seat to speak closer.

"We do not simply wish that you...wrangle the cuckoo. We also wish that you return the egg. Do not attempt to...hatch it yourself. But return the egg. That is important above all other concerns aside from taking care of the bird who took it. Find the cuckoo, clip its wings, and return with the precious egg."

Find the thief, kill them before they can sell or use the virtuous name. And above the rest, bring back the name.

"I can fulfill that condition."

"I have no doubt you can," Third Minister sat back with a contented sigh. "And as to the...ah...intact nature of our precious egg—?"

"It will be intact, returned to you as it was taken. You have my word as a representative of my profession and on my life."

"Good, good. It's just that...so many would be tempted to...try and bring out the chick for their own nests. It is a powerful temptation. For any man or woman. Short of a god's resolve to resist, I should think."

Don't read and take on the name for yourself. But you may be too weak to resist, even a great thiefkiller of low repute like yourself, for all your talk of honor and life. A sidestepping verbal insult against him, one perfectly formed to sound more like a compliment of his resolve than a poke of a worded stick into it, if he were to try and raise issue with it.

Against his professional reserves, Pon-Chai was now quickly tiring and becoming pearl-itched by the grit of the superficial politeness the Third Minister oozed and powdered around him, like a woman's cosmetics clouding the breathable air between them.

"My father would have said something about that as well, good minister."

"Oh?"

"Leave the living to be raised...leave the dead to rise."

"Is that a quote?"

"Yes. From the Great Poet Pon-Chai's collected works."

"Ah, yes." The Third Minister tried to recover with an ungainly nod and false sincerity of understanding in his eyes. "Of course, of course. The Great Poet Pon-Chai. I should have recognized his sage poesy immediately." A glance down at his coffee cup. "Have a love of poetry, have you?"

"No more than any other schoolboy forced to read the Great Works when he'd rather have been out playing in the creek with the others."

Third Minister nodded, chuckled. He lifted up his coffee to sip, immediately grimacing. "*Agh*, it has grown cold."

Pon-Chai rose and stepped back from his chair. "I will leave you to your coffee then."

"Already? You have no other questions or conditions?"

Pon-Chai shook his head. "I have my own manner of making any necessary inquiries. I will contact you for another meeting when I have completed the task."

"As you expressed earlier...it has already been three days. All parties concerned are...most anxious to make sure the egg is returned safe and sound, as soon as possible."

"I understand."

"Are you certain you wouldn't like a fresh cup before you leave? A hot drink for the cold road back home?"

Pon-Chai paused. It had taken the better part of the next day to arrive in time for the hastily-arranged meeting. But today in this district it was warm and muggy, a sudden turn of weather from what it had been out in the suburb where he resided. As far as he knew, only his region near the foothills of Tendo had gotten any cold weather the last couple of days.

Was the minister making a subtle note that, despite all Pon-Chai's precautions and proxies, the thiefkiller's real home location was known to him?

Stupid, he chided himself. Stupid to have quoted his namesake and risking giving away a hint that it was his own virtuous name.

He decided not to push. He didn't like politicians or bureaucrats or their word games. He merely gave that twist-twist polite refusal gesture of his head once more, and left the minister to his coffee.

That rainy yesterday, at Pon-Chai's estate in the suburb. Under a fast, hard watering that had come down like a hermit from the foothills and decided to weep its loneliness over his and his distant neighbors' grounds. The whole house empty except for him and his mother for he had no servants to clean or treat him or his mother. He did the tasks needing done around his own home, relishing the possessiveness he felt it earned him to feel for everything about his estate. A house that smelled always of fresh well-water and dried flowers, like mint and camphor in the vicinity of his mother's chambers, like bread and buttered noodles in the kitchen, and like lavender and sleeping roses in his rooms.

Yesterday, and a repeat of his mother's talk. The same talk after luncheon with the woman who had birthed him, who had her own rooms on the second floor of the large home and had stayed with him since the death of her husband ten years prior.

The same disappointed talk. Held forth as nearly every other of the talks from her seat at the fireplace in the reading room, her blankets wrapped shawl-style about her shoulders and across her lap for additional warmth against the chill that tried to sneak in every time a door opened to allow it, as if they owned housecats of winter air.

She started it with one of the more common vollies, asking him for pen and something to write on.

"Mother, your hands are unsteady. You know that when you use pen and paper now you only give yourself a headache."

She huffed. "There's nothing wrong with my handwriting."

"Perhaps. But what did you want to write, anyway?"

"Maybe my memoirs."

"I would be happy to have you dictate them to me. Then I could not only write them down for you, I would hear and learn quite a bit myself."

She pshawed this. Put a tea cracker in her mouth to crunch it with porcelain teeth. She was not old, but she had aged. Swallowed and chased it with a sip of tea.

"You were named for a poet," his mother spoke as if every word were a lemon rind against her tongue. "The greatest poet of the 47th dynasty, perhaps of all times." She shifted in the chair, looking up at him with wet eyes. "Why did you not follow in your father and namesake's great fields? Why not a writer or poet? With all your travels, you could at least have become a journalist."

"Because I didn't want to be those things." Pon-Chai sat in the opposing chair, equally padded and cushioned, and allowed himself at last to relax slightly. He'd only been home from his last assignment a week and it took those several days to fully arrive back at resting state whenever he came home. "We've had this discussion a thousand different ways and it ends up the same."

"If we've had this discussion a thousand different ways then it ended a thousand different ways. You just refuse to acknowledge the truth of it a different way every time." His mother rearranged the blanket on her lap. "Sixteen years."

"Yes," he sighed. "Sixteen years. Sixteen years saving your dowry and my father's salaries, scrimping and saving so you could afford to buy the name Pon-Chai for me. I know."

"That name was to assure you of an auspicious life."

"A name is little more than a slave collar in life."

"A name is a way of being assured of who you are."

"Your actions are how you assure who you are."

"Or perhaps I don't give you enough credit," his mother said. This was new and it silenced him to hear her out. "Perhaps you became a poet after all."

"How so, mother?"

"A poet whose couplets are a coupling of death with the victim."

The words came like a snap of sparks from one of the logs on the fire. He stared at her for long, dry-throated beats of his heart.

He got up from his seat quickly and silently, deciding that some fresh air out on the rear kitchen porch would be the greatest thing in the world just then. And the kitchen porch was the farthest distance from the reading room he could go without actually leaving the house.

*

What is your name, young man?

Pon-

No! You hear, but do not listen! Your virtuous name you must never give to anyone! Give your professional name, your social name, but never your virtuous one! Now what is your name here?

My name is...is Pupil Aspen.

Better. And what is your social name?

Child...Author Child Aspen.

Better still. Remember that your virtuous name was one your parents labored hard to have bestowed on you. It is the name that holds a ribbon wound directly to your heart, to your brain, to your spirit. Your virtuous name gives hold of that ribbon to any you let hear it who can speak it after. Do you hear me now?

Yes.

And what is my name here?

Tutor Lemonleaf.

Good. Only your parents and your greatest betrothed should ever have your virtuous name. They may have it, and the Recorder General who bestowed it to you. Your name was not cheaply had, child. It should not be cheapened by you giving it away to whomever asks, as careless as a man with holes in his pockets and holes in his brain.

Yes.

*

The smells of wood polish and old dust. Papers. The acrid smell of ink from the pens. All of it dissipated in rain-stench and the clatter of drops collecting, fattening, dropping from weak spots in the crossbeams overhead.

Pon-Chai leaned against one of the porch's columns, resting his forehead against the cool, varnished wood. Just beyond the eaves of the house, the rain came down and the rich petrichor stench hung about the bushes like smoke. His eyes glanced up and happened upon a small, perfect spider's web hanging in the upper corner where the porch column at the far corner of the porch met one of the crossbeams of the roof under the eaves. A few drops of condensation had collected there and caught the failing daylight which is how his eyes had happened on it.

He considered the glitter of the web for long minutes with the rain making a pale curtain of shushing all around.

A poet whose couplets are a coupling of death with the victim. He blinked, rubbed his eyes. For a moment he had the familiar wish that he was made of confectioner's sugar, a sugar shell that could be washed away with the rain like any icicle in spring thaw.

"The temple bell stops," he whispered to the cobweb, to the rain, to the smells in the air, *"but I still hear the sound coming out of the flowers."*

Another poetry quote. One that dated back much, much farther than the first Pon-Chai in the 47th dynasty. The name of that author was lost to much record, as so many great names were lost in the trample of so many cultures of the world over the millennia. Every single one of them rising, rising, like a wave building but never curling into the fist of the slamming tide; a shore of time constantly waiting in ever-deeper-held breath.

*

All those cities out there. All those provinces, nations, districts, Empires, kingdoms, municipalities, even a rare couple of square hectares somewhere that had never seen a flag placed in its stones or any declaration of sovereignty cried out over its waters...places to be other than here. Why be a thiefkiller—even a well-respected one—in his one provincial corner of the larger world?

It wasn't the money, though his fees had certainly made for a comfortable life away from the cities for his mother and himself. There were others who charged higher fees and used *màgique*, and had far lesser success rates to claim for their reputations. Such was the nature of an existence where you could conjure miracles and curses all on the softest glottal hinges of a name. Just a name. The virtuous and true name.

A person or a building, an institution or even a city, even a royal dynasty. All tied to a name. Names hidden away on scrolls in a library of teeming papyri. Names whispered into the ear of a woman with her tongue removed.

Or even branded against the flesh of a single citizen hidden away somewhere behind terra cotta tiled walls. He knew that was outlawed, but still in good practice in smaller hamlets that constantly defied the cartomancers into faithfully plotting on maps of the fringe lands. Putting the town's virtuous name on the living skin of one of its own and then hiding them away, keeping them fed and prisoner to the town's prosperity so no outsider could ever know the true name of this one small but well-done village as they passed through on their way to one of the greater cities. So instead they would be referred to by their traveler names. They became places like Up the Young River and The Town of Five Orange Trees. Others might have transient wonders and for a decade or so be known as The Village of the Fire Juggler or Throat Dancer Village.

Still others might so anger the cartomancers trying to get them in place in time for the release of the new five year's atlas that the m'agique mapmakers would get petty revenge by giving them names to discourage trade and travelers. So one could open up a copy of the Imperial Roads & Ways and at any given edition in its two-hundred-and-forty-six-years run to find fringe villages with names like Dirtwater, The Town of Filthy Troughs, or Whores Township.

Pon-Chai smiled to think that that last one, while perhaps a damning assail to some poor overworked map-inker in the offices of the Empire's Mapsmiths, that last might actually improve a town's trade and travel.

*

Every five years, he dutifully bought a copy of the official atlas.

Anyone who looked at the copies he owned might think it was for his work. But secretly it was the foundation of his one true vice: he collected and sought out ever older editions; as of this new year he would have acquired the last one hundred and thirty consecutive years' worth of releases, all sixteen of them.

Because it was like opening onto that actual period of his land's history. Because of the smell of the faded red and black and blue and green inks, iron and arsenide and cotton-blood tints. Because of the yellowing pages and to open any two random editions to the same sections and see what towns had changed names. What towns had perhaps paid bribes to the Mapsmith offices and gotten better-sounding titles. What places had disappeared.

His mother wondered where he went between his commissions. And that was only for his knowing: he used the older editions to find places to compare to the newer ones. And every time he discovered a place that had no longer rated to be listed as existing according to the mapmakers, he planned and took a trip—alone, no valet, no retinue, no warning or advance note or left-behind instructions to his mother—to find those disappeared haunts.

Many of them were only that: haunts. The forest- or desert-reclaimed remnants of a village that had fallen to the deaths of time or conquest or commerce and human boredom.

Sometimes in these dead places, if he found a particularly beautiful sight—a broken-down church with no roof filled with apple blossoms in the autumn, or a toucan tree growing out of a house with its many-colored blooms on full display—he would sit and watch it for hours. Memorizing it. Taking it in for every detail he could possibly commit to his thoughts. Not composing, not seeking words to make a mental diary, not sketching. All things his father would have done.

But the way Pon-Chai interpreted things, his father had commodified everything by being a writer before being a human. His sire had reduced all wonder and horror, all that color and flavor, to artful words and careful syllabically-balanced compositions of tales. Powerful, to be sure, but powerful in the sense of evoking those things the way a hired Lightweaver could present a play before a court using spells to conjure thin images of people and things. Not preserving or properly *being* any of them. To his father, everything was a world of writing underneath its cosmetically inconvenient skin of being real, and he'd spent his life's vocation teasing out the words from the skin. Almost more like a trapper, a skin-trader, than an artist. Trying to bring back the meat he tricked out of its pelts and shells.

He was not his father.

He knew this and it seemed he was the only one happy to accept this, if his mother's puzzled complaining was any indication.

A rare one or two of these disappeared places were mapmaker errors for places that still were there in the real world. Omissions, mistakes...and the rarest of these already-scarce examples still thrived but had secreted away their virtuous names so well that the mapmakers could no longer even assign them travel names for their maps.

Almost as if these places wanted to defy people just like his father had been: people who wanted a name and a place and statistics to set down on paper for census-taking and map-making. As if that would somehow define and confine those places to these bits of bare data.

*

In his last thirteen years of thiefkilling, Pon-Chai had only discovered one such place.

The locals there had been surprised to have him walk right into their town by its disused main road, all weeds and unraked gravel left from when the road had once been fine laid stone.

But he was not from any Imperial office and had not been on any official commission for anyone. They ultimately had welcomed him as something they had not seen in nearly seventy years since their village had last appeared in the Maps & Ways book: a tourist.

He spent nearly two weeks there before returning home. Sleeping in a different house each night as the household's guest. Hearing them tell stories (most of these nothing remarkably new...minor variations on what were otherwise standard child fables and cautionary adult tales).

He finally after three nights got to sample their special cold soup that was shockingly hot with spices after the diner let it rest on their tongue and experience its oddly walnut-and-bananas flavor for a moment. Then the burn would flare up like a phoenix rising from the ashes of the palate, and like fresh whiskey would take that burn all the way down to the stomach and transform into a long-lasting chemical warmth.

They called it Winter's Chill and prepared gallons of it whenever the seasons grew too cold for lantern-boys to keep their workers warm while working outdoors. It was believed to keep anyone who ate it from being susceptible to any such thing as hypothermia no matter how freezing the winter snows that collected round them.

The secret, one of the younger cooks had giggled and confided to him when he smiled at her, redfaced and puffing from finishing his first bowl, was a small pepper shaped like a rhino horn and the color of cow's blood. They only grew on some hillsides near that village and were collected every year and first soaked in ginger sauce for a week. Then they were taken out and strung up like a string of unlit firecrackers and allowed to dry for no less than a year before being used in the soup.

*

"*The drying is the real trick,*" she said, unselfconsciously pushing back a loose strand of bright copper hair that had come loose of her server's bun. "*You have to have years of experience to learn how to read the peppers.*"

He stopped swallowing down the warm milk she'd given him to ease the burning and goggled at her wetly. "*Read the peppers?*"

"*Mm-hmm. It takes a skilled eye to know how to look at the peppers on the strings and know which ones are truly dried and ready for use, and which ones need to hang a little longer. A certain way that the old women can look and feel the wrinkles in a pepper to know how long it's dried there. A pepper that's cooked before it's fully dry is a waste. You don't truly get warm when you make the soup from it.*"

*

Over the days, he'd come to know several of the villagers more personally even though he never learned anything approaching the village's virtuous name. The young cook was Little Second-Chef Bandole. By the end of his stay, he called her by their own friendnames for each other: he called her Bandy, and she called him Aspic because she said his social name reminded her of the meat jelly they cooked down from stock for holiday meals.

He could not make any map of his own of course. Any attempt to do so would find the ink snarled, the lines washed away as he blinked, any words written to give a name to the place becoming a scribble of meaningless marks. But he had his own travel-name for the village. The natives called it nothing more than "home" or "here," since none of them had any need to refer to it by its virtuous name out loud or explain to each other where they were.

He called it "Peaceful."

*

Pon-Chai noted the slackening of the rainfall even as twilight proper arrived and set some soaked birds to twittering in the nearby trees.

When he squinted, his eyes were sharp enough to see a series of golden pinpricks, one lighting then the next, in a slanted line. The lanterns of his nearest neighbor's front drive. *M'agique* lanterns, charmed to flare their wicks to spectral light when the sun fell beyond the foothills. It was a bit unsettling to see lanterns light themselves, one after another rather than all at once. Lighting in sequence made it seem as if there was some physical agency going from each to the next, invisible but trudging the length of the drive in the weakening rain. One unseen light, catching the oil-soaked wicks to flame and then retiring to some charm-scratched cage in the aether. His own lanterns were dark, lit the old fashioned way but only if he expected visitors.

He went back inside to discover he was chilled without having even noticed it until the bread oven warmth of the house wrapped around him.

His mother would be asleep on her early evening nap in the chair where he'd left her. She was a restless sleeper and only managed a few hours at a time. By middle of the night, he'd be able to hear her shuffles and creaks as she went down to the kitchen and made herself fresh coffee, or honeyed tea to settle a stomach that was quiet less and less each day.

All around him, as he stood in the back hall that led from the kitchen's rear porch to the front rooms, he took in a silence that was almost conspiratorial. Like walking in from the rain, he'd interrupted a louder conversation where people in the house had been talking about him.

He knew that such things were not always merely the calm cricks and ticks of the house warping in the weather.

Sometimes, those whispers in the corners really were whispers.

Underneath the house, in the soil of its crawlspace chambers that honeycombed its foundation, the ashes of his father were scattered before the first stones had been laid to build this place.

And his father had come from a large family.

While he had the respite of his mother's napping, Pon-Chai decided it was time to open the note on dark crimson paper that he'd received earlier that day from a footboy. A new commission, with him only a week returned from the last.

Perhaps it was what he truly needed, he considered, breaking the wax seal. To not have to think too much about the rain, his mother. And poetry lost to him as surely as a village disappeared off the Imperial maps.

After he left the coffeehouse, he took the usual first countermeasures against being followed, leaving as he'd come but immediately doubling back and taking a more circuitous twist of route around the next few buildings before going back towards the main street.

His habitual cautions were rewarded. As he gained the open market at the square at the opposite end of the street from the coffeehouse, he found what he'd previously scanned in the market: the pewter trader. Here was even more tarnished and tawdry samples of metalwork, but at least unlike the Third Minister and his subdued coffeehouse there was no pretending to anything better for sale. The merchant himself even bowed his head and said nothing as Pon-Chai inspected the bottoms of large cooking bowls and mixing bowls with the careful gravity of a jewel cutter.

And saw the two shadows that Third Minister Adjunct-Willow had no doubt had trailing him since he'd left their meeting. One was hovering near a fruit vendor, the other was seemingly lounging over an old bookseller's table of junk volumes. But both shared the same furtive fox's head turns, always somehow ignoring the wares in front of them in favor of glancing in his direction. A particularly vivid-bright finished mixing bowl's bottom gave him the crucial intelligence before he set it aside.

"Are these true pewter, or the new industrial alloy that mixes in antimony and steel edges?"

The merchant shook his head. "I am only one small collectibles dealer. These are classic, unglazed and unstained. None is newer than six years, I know that much."

Pon-Chai nodded. Between his hands was a bowl deeper than it was wide, about the diameter of a robin's nest but deep enough he could have served a broth luncheon to four people with it as his serving dish. It didn't glitter as the coffeehouse service had, but rather the light rolled along its battered surfaces even as he rolled it between his hands.

He hesitated only a moment, one finger tapping the bowl's underside. "I will give you five and a half."

The merchant shook his head. "The asking price is seven, sir. This is not a haggling district."

Pon-Chai gave the man his unblinking stare for a few sacrificed seconds. The merchant tried to smile and look him in those creekbed rounded-stone eyes. But somewhere in the process his face muscles seemed to lose the knack of how to make the expression, and instead he nodded again. "Yes, sir."

Pon-Chai paid him the offered price, a tinkling of small change. The bowl had two welded handles—barely big enough to be suitable for a baby's play-set of such utensils—and he used a piece of twine from one of his inner pockets to secure the bowl by tying it via one of its handles to his belt sash. It swung there like a strange codpiece until he noticed and pulled his sash so that the bowl swung to his left hip and out of the way of his step.

Two shadows. The Third Minister was not a man who believed in the failures of redundancy. Good enough.

Pon-Chai saw the opening in the crowd to the south of the square, and made his movements toward it. His shadows broke away too fast from their posts and took to following.

He lost them in less than five minutes' time, using his real countermeasures and actually leaving the city by canal to the west and then back to the Steel Road which would eventually lead out of Gheru and to his suburb estate. He noted as he paid the canal boatmaster for the short ride a small professional pleasure that his real countermeasures were still perfectly effective, as opposed to the first kind that were useless for hiding one's trail but excellent for forcing out the presence of anyone following.

The contract had begun in earnest. And it had begun as all his contracts must: with the distrust of the client.

*

As with all such contracts, he did not return completely to home, but at the way station he had set up about a third of the distance back. A far humbler and smaller residence, not new-built but bought during one of the many periodic reconstruction and gentrification phases in the village of Twining Ivy Traps, the last major hamlet before the open grounds and country roads where he and his mother lived.

A single-story brick affair, buried at the end of the service alley amidst an old manufacturing precinct of Twining Ivy Traps that saw very little day to day traffic other than the delivery of materials to clothing makers and reeds to those who still sold 'artisanal hand made' wicker baskets and similar crafts. There were machine shops in the larger cities that mass produced cheaper and sometimes even better items with great variety of colors and sizes. But Pon-Chai, as in many of his choices, enjoyed places where people still invested themselves in their work. It also meant less attention paid to this tiny end-of-alley former paymaster's office that he'd converted to his own private workspace.

He checked the fine wire catches on the door as he entered. Undisturbed. Another few minutes were spent quietly inspecting the two front windows and the one tiny rear window over the toilet, and these too were found to have remained safe.

There were other ways he could've used. *M'agique* afforded a number of varying degrees of property security when employed discriminately. There were etch-charms that could be embedded in the sills of every window, or pao-tadusz gold plates one could have regularly recharged by a priest and nailed above the doorways. Ways to make it so would-be thieves didn't notice the building at all. Or if they did, would find themselves confused and unable to concentrate while attempting to pick the locks or take a chisel to one of the window frames.

But every charm had a counter-charm. Every curse could backfire as the holding sigils wore and faded. Better a solid black-painted wire or two to safeguard a well-left space than to worry constantly about the failings of a conjuration.

He could hear the whirring of looms in the next-door millinery. Soothing. He sat at his writing desk (setting the cheap pewter bowl down on its top shelf as he did so) and simply listened to the sound for some time.

*

There are many others who use m'agique and tricks to accomplish their goals. And that might be fine for getting the washing done before it rains, or making sure the bread doesn't burn in the oven. But we do not rely on it for the things that matter.

Yes, sir.

You can use someone's social name or professional name and a tracking charm to try and get a lead on where they've gone, but that's useless if they've decided to truly abandon their past. Or if they operate under so many false-names that any one of them is meaningless. Or if they have adopted a common name, like some lowly Untaught, to blend into the crowds. Are you hearing me?

Yes, sir. We don't use m'agique.

Exactly. We use detection. *We use* guile. *We use* blade *and* wire *and* poison. *We use our eyes to find and our hands, if all else fails. But do your work well, and rarely should anything fail on you. You are your own greatest set of tools, Aspen. Never let that lesson above all else leave you.*

Thank you, Killer Master Three Brooms.

Just Brooms is fine.

A...

What?

Is that...would that be a friend-name *between us, sir?*

Sure. If your teacher is not your friend, what good is what they're teaching you? An enemy can never mentor you in anything but your own defeats, after all.

Th-thank you s—

Brooms.

Thank you, Brooms.

*

He checked that his paperwork was up to date. All the property and estate arrangements, the trusts established for his mother's care in the event he didn't return. There were people he trusted who would come to this place and execute his testament if he didn't contact them in a certain timeframe.

Everything appeared to still be in order, so he closed and locked up the writing desk and hid the key in its hidey hole dug out under the plaster in the toilet.

He reviewed his cabinets. It took longer than he'd expected.

A Royal contract. Through proxy after proxy, true, but a contract that led to the highest office in the nation, nonetheless. He had interrogated and probed in situations that involved bureaucracies and high parties in the past...but never at this level.

Third Minister had offered to let him ask questions, but following his experience he had declined. The answers you gathered were usually of a better quality than the ones delivered to your door, much like cooking your own meals versus going to some dingy café.

And when considering those two foxy shadows he'd abandoned back in the square...any answers he got by that way would have been a twisted path of half-truths and protective lies to limit culpability for certain parties, no doubt. There would be executions in the Palace Golden this following week already...certainly nobody including the Third Minister wanted to add their names to the list of heads needing removing.

So how to prepare for an investigation and tracking that involved the Royal imprimatur all over it?

Time...time was slipping with every hour.

"Three days," he breathed.

He'd have to start with the likeliest place to find true information. That wouldn't be anywhere near the court or its houses of government functionaries. The court would either close its many doors to him at the first misspoken question, or give him nothing but cotton and twine for his trouble...no real ribbon to the truth and the thief wrapped within it.

He pushed aside his finer robes and traveling clothes, and instead looked to his cheapest woolens and dirty silks.

"Fifty was what your girl quoted me."

Pon-Chai didn't make eye contact with either of the two men who sat at equidistant seats at the round table he had taken in the back of the establishment.

The place smelled of fish oil and old grease; every surface had a waxy, overripe fruitskin feeling to the finger's touch. Pon Chai tried to only be in contact with his lone cup of watered-down peach-and-honey tea, and kept his overlong sleeves from resting on the table top.

"She tends to be too friendly for the sake of keeping business," the one on his right said, giving a gap-toothed smile. While it never paid to assume based on appearances, he had a guttural voice and manner of carrying himself, in contempt of everything around him with smiling dismissal, that suggested he was an Untaught. One of the many illiterate proletarian masses of the cities.

Pon-Chai sometimes nearly envied these types of people. They were poor, many living on the constant razor's edge of outright starvation and disease. The Untaught were that sub-stratum of the world that actually reveled in refusing to learn to read or write any of the official languages.

It was a paper-thin joke to think any of these people could afford virtuous names of any merit. Instead they took two-penny names and they were, as one kingdom saying went, a dime-a-dozen. This one here with the garden-fence smile was probably named something like Thom or Bai or Pak, a name shared by who knew how many others and often only differentiated by a secondary name from his home district or even, for former convicts, his prisoner ward number-name.

But oh, what a kind of freedom that gave them all. Such cheaply-had names were so frequent, so common, that *m'agique* to track or assault any people amongst these hordes was a waste of conjuring.

"She's a good saleswoman," the other to his right picked up the thread of the conversation. "But overly enthusiastic." He did not share his partner's smile, which told Pon-Chai he was the one to consider truly dangerous. "The price is one hundred and thirty. *And*," his voice betrayed only the slightest humor as he used the old merchant's line, "this is not a haggling district."

An old bandit's trap. If he tried to argue, they would quickly rise to put down his debate, either with louder voices or straight to violence. If he agreed, they knew he had the money and would simply rob him at the first convenient chance.

He tried the middle gambit, knowing it was futile but feeling obliged to at least meet the formality.

"I'm afraid I only came prepared to pay the fifty she quoted me. Then I guess I was misinformed. Sorry to have wasted your time." He pushed back from the table without rising.

"Excuse me," the smiler to the left said, "but we didn't say that we were done here. And as you've just pointed out for us, our time is valuable. Whether we do business or not."

"Gentlemen," Pon-Chai kept his voice smooth and calm, as if utterly oblivious to any risk. "I appreciate the difficulty, but if the price was inaccurately quoted, I'm afraid I don't have anything I can offer you."

The men exchanged a glance. The smiler glanced past his companion's shoulder, to take in the room beyond them and see if anyone was particularly paying any attention this way. The place was busy but only comparably so: all but the last few tables towards the rear were taken by other customers. The front serving boys were busy bustling from the kitchen to the front tables. Everywhere was the dovecote murmur of the others, but nothing boisterous.

Pon-Chai would have preferred a louder place, more boisterous, but his meeting companions through their proxy had insisted on meeting after midnight, and while the place was a popular tea-and-dumplings house near the canals it wasn't serving any hard spirits to warrant too many noisome patrons to help provide cover.

The serious one leaned forward. "You aren't getting our point. We're not leaving here without something for our trouble."

Pon-Chai opened his hands from around his cooling tea cup, gently waving them inwards towards the cup to indicate it. "I'm truly, truly sorry, sirs. Other than this cup of tea in front of me, I haven't a thing on me to satisfy you."

The smiler chuckled and reached forward, plucking up the cup of tea from between Pon-Chai's hands. He tipped it back and downed it in a couple of fast swallows. Made theatrical smacking and sighing sounds as he clunked the cup down, chipping the porcelain of the cup's rim bottom. Pon-Chai watched this while letting his hands fall back into his lap.

"Cheap tea," the smiler remarked to his companion. Then to Pon-Chai: "You said you came prepared to pay fifty. So we're thinking fifty is about what our wasted time here has been worth. And whatever else you may be truly carrying on you."

Pon-Chai frowned, looking down and raising his opened hands in staged apology.

"I'm sorry that we seem to be at an impasse."

"No," the serious one said immediately. "*You* have reached an *impasse*. My partner and I. You won't pass us at all, until we get our due. And for wasting our time further with this whining, the rate goes up in what we'll...take out as ours." The serious one leaned to his side slightly enough to make clear to Pon-Chai's line of sight the dagger nestled inside the line of his sash belt.

Pon-Chai's frown permitted out a faint sigh of air. "It is cheap tea. But honey at least is plentiful enough in this season. And honey in peach tea is good for covering the faint taste of the spider-bark powder."

The smiler froze. "What're you talking about?"

"In that cup of tea of mine that you so rudely slurped down your fat throat. A spoonsful of spider-bark powder. It tastes very weakly of something like...salty cinnamon, I'm told. The honey covers it up just fine for my purposes. In about a minute you'll notice your tongue and lips going numb. At some point after that...depending on your digestion...your lungs should stop remembering how to breathe in and out."

The smiler's face went to a dull bronze as he looked to his partner, who had already reached to put his hand on his dagger's handle, eyes darting around the room to take another survey of the occupants.

He rallied back a laugh. "You must think we're true fools. That was your cup, why would you poison your own tea?"

"You're right that the tea here is quite execrable. I was using it to warm my hands and have something to occupy them, not to drink. And while you were chuckling and talking about your valuable time, you weren't paying attention to my hands rubbing the sides of the cup, were you? Of course you weren't. Or you would have noticed how my right palm seemed to slide a little higher and over the rim at one point. Or how I then swished the cup around. To better stir in the powder."

"You're lying," the serious one said, as if saying the thing would make it so. "You couldn't know either of us would drink it."

"Ah, well, for that you may be right. There is no predicting the future, even though charlatan tea-leaf romancers claim to. But I've had a while to study all types of people. And many people's behaviors are as predictable as dropping a stone in a bucket and knowing it will sink. Very rarely do you get surprised with a floating stone. And your friend here," Pon-Chai regarded the smiler, "unfortunately for him, he very much sank to the bottom as expected."

"You know anything about this stuff?" the smiler demanded of his partner.

"Give him the cure," the serious one hissed. "Or you die screaming with my metal in your belly."

"A cure?" Pon-Chai frowned deeper, tilting his head to consider the request. "Do you mean an antidote? Oh, I understand you fine. There isn't one. Spider-bark powder is a cyanotic mixture, each batch prepared as a unique recipe by its preparer. In this case, I made that batch myself. And I added a pinch of distilled tobacconite from the southerlands. Even if you got your friend here to vomit right now, the spider-bark will have already made its way into his bloodstream thanks to the heightened circulation the tobacconite extract excites in the system."

"I can't...! Umm!" The smiler's mouth was now hanging open. No longer smiling. A glisten of drool began to drop from a corner of the lips. *"Guhm!"* His eyes were wide open, the yellowed whites shining like nicotined folds of newspaper. His mouth was clearly incapable of further speech. He tried to rise, but there was a horrid whistling gasp from his mouth and he fell back to his seat.

"Oh...I take it you didn't eat before coming? An empty stomach would account for such a fast followup response after the numbness." Pon-Chai watched the men in their seats. The smiler now simply slackening, his eyes the only thing that seemed to still be active and nerved to alertness but helplessly staring back as his chest rose and fell with ever-more labored breathing. The serious one was a statue of hand on dagger handle, looking at his partner and Pon-Chai in savagely sharp jerks of his head. He seemed to be chewing on his lower lip in consideration.

"Give me the money then," the serious one finally said. "And I walk out. You can deal with this," he tilted his forehead towards the gasping one, "yourself."

Pon-Chai furrowed his lips, regarding the serious one carefully.

About three and three-quarter feet from me.

Leading with the right foot.

But his dagger hand is his left.

He'll try and turn to conceal it as he moves forward. That would put him off balance.

He'll want to come around the edge of the table rather than more efficiently shoving it over and making a commotion.

He's darker-skinned than his partner...but there is blonde in the strawberry of his hair and his eyes are green. A halfbreed? Perhaps from Forshem Region... used to much warmer climate than in the royal cities...he's wearing an extra layer under his tunic, an undershirt or some wool slip.

"Not much of a partnership, I should say," he remarked. "Willing to just walk out on your friend for a handful of coins as his life seeps away?"

A tiny click as the dagger came out from its home, but the serious one kept his wrist bent in, the blade pointed towards himself rather than wave it around for all to see.

"Give me the money." Now there was the shake, the tiniest waver in the voice.

Pon-Chai stared at the man. Their eyes stayed fixed, even as the sound of a final desperate, clipped breath drafted in the space between them.

Pon-Chai did not blink. Did not smile. Did not offer any further witticisms.

"You will not receive any money from me for your treachery," he spoke in the slow tones of a man proclaiming an oncoming storm to the owner of a fleet of ships at sea. "You will, if you survive, perhaps be a little less Untaught from this lesson."

In seemingly one single quicksilver movement:

Pon-Chai's left leg rose, the lower half smoothly curling in like a mantis' foreleg as it gathered its speed to spear a smaller insect.

As soon as his calf muscle met the back of his thigh, the leg immediately flexed out, the foot deftly curving slightly at the ankle as the leg swung forward and inward to the right...and the ball of his heel with all the force of his leg found the back of the serious one's hand holding the dagger against his own stomach.

A tearing sound of fabric. The squashing noise like stepping into a spoiled melon. The grunt-wheeze of a sucked-in breath of shocking, cold-swallowing pain.

Pon-Chai's leg snapped back to its original position. All of this without even raising the front legs of his chair from the table or disturbing his hands resting in his lap.

And without ever breaking eye contact.

The serious one's face went as slack as his dying friend next to him. But his mouth managed to show a pale pink tongue that rolled against the yellowed lower teeth. It was as if his tongue, having learned the foolishness of the rest of the body housing it, was probing for a path to escape. The total effect was a look of disbelief.

"Your metal is in your belly, sir," he said quietly. "If you leave now, perhaps by the back porch of this establishment, you may still have time to find someone who can tend to the worst of the wounds before you bleed to death."

In the rush of movement as the serious one whimpered, rose, his chair not quite tilting enough to fall over as he whirled and stumbled for the back door, Pon-Chai bent forward, a hand flying forward to the smiler's face. Two swift fingertips lightly grasped their pads to the eyelids of the dead man and pushed them closed over the eyes. The gentlest exertion of pressure before lifting his fingertips secured the lids down in the gum of the dead man's last terrified tears.

There was not even a telltale trail of blood drops to give away any wrongdoing. The serious one's extra layer of clothing had absorbed the first seizure of blood to come from his wound. At least long enough to see him out the back porch.

"Sir?" The serving boy arrived to the commotion of the other's leaving, pointed to the dead man. "Is your friend all right?" The boy nodded to the empty cup. "Was there something wrong with his tea?"

"Not at all," Pon-Chai left a clatter of coins on the tabletop, enough to pay the bill and leave a fair tip. "The tea was exceptional. My friend tends to nod off after a good, hot cup is in his belly." The thiefkiller smiled at the serving boy. "Do let him have his small nap for a while, would you? He's been overworked of late and our time here was his first break in days."

The serving boy bowed, not looking any further. He thanked Pon-Chai for his business as the thiefkiller left in no rush by the front entrance.

*

During his next hour of moving about to get to his temporary apartment, he was shocked at one point to go down what had been previously checked as a simple trash alley and find a beggar woman he nearly ran into. She was trying to make her small living shaking a dirty, cracked cup.

The sight of the woman, disheveled and covered with wrinkles of dust and cracked grime to the degree that she almost seemed sun-dried, leather-tanned, caught him like a fishhook snagging a fisherman's sleeve. He was helpless to slow down and talk to her, amidst the rotten piles of rain-sotted papers, shattered crates and discarded foods (and worse).

"A penny?" She shook her cup more with a palsy than any emphasis, raising it to her head height where she sat, cross-legged and hunched, atop a small pile of flattened wood slats collected from various crates and boxes. When her cup shook, it made no sound.

No coins, not even shills to encourage charity.

He looked back and forth along the ends of the alley.

He stared down at her, unblinking, as she shook her cup and repeated her plea.

He closed his eyes and listened.

There was some caterwauling from a baby somewhere in the floors above them. There was the sound of a couple arguing (or lovemaking with angry abandon, it was all the same). He couldn't hear the trying-to-be-silent footfalls of anyone trailing him.

He opened his eyes and looked down at the beggar woman with a fresh look. Trying to see...

There could be a knife in that sleeve.

No coins in the cup.

Then he saw that the woman's odd posture in her cross-legged position was because she was missing her left foot, at least a goodly part of it to mid-arch. It looked smooth and unscarred, suggesting a birth deformity not a trauma.

He frowned, trapped in the moment.

This is an out-of-the-way alley for begging.

The foot meant nothing, wrapped in a ragged swaddling of filth-blackened cotton ragging. Three Brooms had walked with a severe limp. A souvenir of one of his last contracts; he'd never said more about it, but had never said it was souvenir of his *last* contract. He had been a capable man in this field well before physical limits had argued for him becoming a dark teacher.

An out-of-the-way alley, yes. There was nobody else back here. But by the same token, Pon-Chai knew that in the city's bowels, begging and pickpocketing were pushed to being the work of cutthroat cousins to the bandits he'd dispatched back in the eatery. To be a beggar on a major city street was not only to duck and dodge the eye of city magistrates or nightwatch patrols, but to also avoid the knives of your competitor beggars. Or the self-styled Tomcat Princes who led small bands of beaten, cowed children with hungry animal eyes to pick someone clean of their goods and even clothes faster than the legend of a school of *pikhana* fish swarming and flensing cattle clean of flesh. To be a beggar of any standing in a city as major as the royal principalities, one would be expected to be barely a step below highwayman in strength, speed and willingness to kill. Or better to be weak but in a group, as any bundle of sticks resisting snapping.

She could just as easily have been alone in this dingy alley where nobody could be truly expected to walk by, much less with any money to spare, as a matter of the stratified realities of life amongst the many Common Named and Untaught.

"A penny? Perhaps two, for a gentleman as you look?" Her voice was clear, however, and her eyes did not squint. She looked hard worn but not broken down. "I am wanting to buy a little bread, and save for a name."

Pon-Chai gave his faint smile, still unblinking. "You seem a bit old, pardon me, to have not yet been before a Recorder General."

The woman shook her head, a few strands pulling free of the tatty bun she'd tied it up in. "No, sir, not for me." With a wince, she straightened up slightly, and he could see the bulge of her belly under her patched and soiled tunic.

Pon-Chai glanced at the ends of the alley again. Still no one. He hunched down to bring his eyes level with hers.

"Have you seen a doctor? A chirurgeon? At least some backstreet practicalist, to tell you it's a boy or a girl?"

The woman shook her head. "It is all I can do to make enough to feed myself. Myself and my little nameless."

He didn't glance down at her half-foot, not wanting her to see the flick of his eyes or feel any embarrassment at him noticing.

He reached into another hidden pocket of his inner breast and withdrew a small coin purse. This was stuffed with scraps of velvet the coins went between to keep them from clinking and jangling against each other.

He looked at the few gold coins in there, a fingertip almost touching the mint-stamped edge. Paused.

No. It is cruel to give gold that would only reflect sun back on this poor target in this dim place.

He closed the coin purse and returned it to his inner pocket. The woman watched, not confused or angry or disappointed, merely waiting for whatever would come.

He reached into a different pocket and pulled out a similar purse, this one slightly larger and heavier. In here were the fifty silvers he had carefully tended and brought with him, intending to pay the men in the eatery for information.

He didn't open the purse, merely handed it to her. She put down her cup into her lap and opened it, looking into it.

"It will not buy you any great name," he said quietly, as she looked up at him. Now very open shock registered on the woman's face and for a moment he could see a gleam (perhaps the famed glow of a pregnant woman?) of something like plain beauty in her features. "But there should be enough there to keep you in bread and milk a while, and to at least go see a midwife once or twice and be sure that the child is coming along healthy."

He was almost to the opposite end of the alley from the way he'd come when her voice caught him, that fishhook once more.

"Why, sir?" A ragged gulp of air that he could hear nearly choked her ability to speak completely, but she cough-cried the rest. "Are you a demon at games with the poor and the hopeless, and this will turn to paper scraps and maggots in the morning?"

He stopped, but did not turn around.

"It will buy you bread and milk for a time. A few drops of honey for sweetness. Take yourself to wherever you sleep now, and get warm. You and your child both."

"What is your name?"

One of the old superstitious gambits amongst the simpler fable-folk: no demon could give you a name, even a false one, or else it risked being held back by a hedge circle. Penny magic, cheap but frustratingly effective if someone could draw out a charm-circle and utter the false-name in time.

And yet any living man can give you whatever name he likes, and a circle or invoke-charm wouldn't make a bit of difference.

"Canto," he answered.

She cried thanks over and over until he was gone and out of earshot, back into the mazes of streets and backways to make sure his path behind was clear.

He changed clothes back in the rented room, a good dozen city blocks from the canals. He would be leaving before dawn, the rent paid through the next night so the hotelier shouldn't come knocking about her guest until well after he was gone.

The better part of a day and a half. Wasted.

He tried to keep frustration from overwhelming him.

He left the discarded clothes in a corner while putting on a fresh set of woolen tunic and pants. From a paper bag under the rude cot was a fresh pair of dry canvas shoes. He collected off the cot everything that had been in his pockets and neatly re-stowed them in the fresh clothing.

A flicker of his foot as he had slipped his left into the new shoe.

Slightly bruised toes. Going to have to be careful I don't sprain them completely if there's another time.

He sat himself on the cot in a similar cross-legged position as the beggar-mother had been in, only rigid-backed and hands resting palms-down on his extended knees.

He pictured a perfect triangle formed by the top of his head, extending down via his arms to his knees, and his crossed legs as the bottom beam of the shape.

A few careful breaths. Slowly turning down the volume of the various tenement noises. Someone talking too loudly and someone else laughing too hard in response overhead. Footsteps. Shuffles. Another baby crying (such a ubiquitous sound in the cities, as if people didn't even have to make love so much as their press and squeezing clutter against each other forced new humans into being in the small spaces left amidst them).

Frustrating. A waste of time.

Think of another way. Unwind the ribbon back to the name of the problem and declare it. Bind it to you.

*

The girl was one of many in the House of Red Chambers and Sweetness. As with all the licensed bordellos he found it in the Courtesanta district. It took him some careful questioning of the fringe drinking houses between Courtesanta and the canals to be sure of which houses were the most popular amongst the palace guard and lower functionaries.

Red Chambers was a relatively modest establishment by the standards of the royal capital. Which was to say that it would have baffled and awed any country merchant with more gold than sense as they walked through its half-moon front doors (and had survived this deep into the city beyond the outer markets without being robbed).

But Pon-Chai had heard his father talk.

There's nothing wrong with them in principle. Some of the nicer ones are downright palatial in their own right. The women are polite, quite beautiful, kept clean and tended and paid well by the house masters.

But...? His mother, arching an eyebrow as they sat at the small dinner table. The child Pon-Chai, perhaps ten years old, sat as always perfectly at the halfway point between them; only alternating randomly from one side or the other of the thin, narrow strip of wood that was the table resting on its trestle legs. He was a bee, quietly sipping from flowers while the winds talked in the trees above.

But no matter how delightful a girl is for you, no matter how simple your pleasures may be to have sated or perfectly they might suit your wants, there is a fashioning there in the eyes. It looks...

His father frowning. The face that looked much as Pon-Chai's did only much more line-stroked, as if Time were a master calligrapher or a *mágique* Pen Dancer, leaving its pretty marks with each year along the edges of the eyes, the mouth. The look that always heralded a frustrating search for the right word, the next perfect phrasing. Even with no paper or pen but a fork and a plate of boiled beef and lentils, his father was writing.

...it looks as mechanical as the clock that is always running in her head. Almost like you can see the hands turn every time her eyes don't quite laugh at your jokes the way her mouth does. Her perfume just makes me think of when it will be washed off later, amongst other things she cleans from both body and memory. There is a falsehood there that doesn't work for me.

Maybe because you're so used to manufacturing your own, his mother answered with a mischievous smile. Pon-Chai looked back at his father at this, but his father merely nodded and went back to eating. Every so often until the meal was done, Pon-Chai looked to his father to see his sire frowning at his plate as he considered further what he was going to write about on this subject, eager to finish with some premise or catch so engrossing that he'd been talking his thoughts aloud at dinner.

Courtesanta was one of those bastard hybrid words, something mish-mashed from one old tongue and another, sounding in a way as imported as a honeymead vintage from the far North Kell kingdoms. The cross-tongue meaning was something of 'the saintly concubine' or even in some gutter slang 'godly prostitutes.'

Whatever the name, he had been able to narrow down to Red Chambers by finding out from a few barkeeps where they often recommended (or were paid off to recommend) that tipsy soldiers go to spend the rest of their hard-earned pay during their short monthly leave-takings of rest. The House of Red Chambers and Sweetness had further proved to be the most popular of the three. Cinnamon Ochre and the Theater of Solemn Sighs were a bit cheaper, yet for this reason many lower functionaries and palace guard preferred Red Chambers as it gave them the best value for their pittance salaries. *As well a hummingbird for two pennies as a dead one for half that, if a man must have a bird regardless,* an old proverb cautioned. When they returned back to their palace roles, these men and women were going to be effectively penniless again until next paymaster reckoning. They may as well, for those who wanted pleasures of flesh over food or drink, get their money's worth. Red Chambers was affordably within their means while still giving them a measure of affluence in their sin-taking.

He'd paid the bouncer at the front room and given the matron his private-social name for this purpose, so she could then go forth into the atrium of the building where the girls sat and giggled or sighed and batted eyes from around a red tile-bottomed half-spherical pool set in the floor.

At the center of the pool which took up much of the atrium not filled with cushions and female flesh, there was a dinner-plate-sized iron column. Atop it, a foot above the water, a small red lacquered box contained a small buzzing beehive. Bees flew in and out lazily, up to the skylights beyond the hanging orange and crimson tapestries. The faintest smell of honey (secretly from incense burned in vents rather than coming from the measly apiary box in the centerpiece) permeated all other scents.

The atrium was eight-sided. One side was the tiny foyer where he'd entered and paid the guard, as the matron had coming smiling to receive him. The opposite end was a matching pair of half-moon doors that led to the inner chambers of the house.

The three sides to the left and right were shallow alcoves with comfortable padded benches where a customer could take whichever empty seat they liked and watch the pool in the center without seeing or disturbing anyone negotiating and talking in one of the other alcoves. As a customer nodded, or waved to a girl at the pool, or had a specifically named one brought to him by the matron when the girl was available, an attendant would silently bring a small rattan screen over to the mouth of the alcove. This allowed privacy and quiet for the necessary period of friendly welcome, some varied degrees of getting to know each other, and finally the negotiations for what would take place beyond the inner doors.

The matron had whispered him the rules of etiquette as he'd followed her into the atrium and then to the first available seat. In the alcoves no business beyond welcome and negotiating was to take place. No brutal treatment of any girl, no abuse or disrespect to anyone representing the house masters. There were a few other minor details about percentages expected as gratuities and 'grateful acknowledgments' for the guards who tended other entries and exits of the house to ensure the safety and discretion of all within.

Pon-Chai nodded and waved the matron away once he took his seat. Once she was gone, he relaxed and stared at the atrium. His eyes found a point in indeterminate space a-ways across the water and just above the apiary box. His mind was using his eyes as a *camera obscura*, a wide-open aperture taking in the details of the whole vista bathed in pink-and-tangerine tints. Missing nothing as he took an unblinking assessment of the dozen girls who lounged around the pool.

The three alcoves across from him were all screened. There was a scattering of titters and laughs, once a harsh seal-bark of a man guffawing away at something sweetly whispered to him.

Some of the girls talked. A few ignored him completely, not even glancing his way since he'd walked into the chamber. Others would bat gilded eyelashes at him, or smile secretive grins under eyes pitted in kohl to look like something sexually feral and borderline threatening. All the fancy for a place that so often catered to soldiers of the palace and often so no more action than patrolling of corridors or the occasional removal of an offending ambassador. The weakest haze of incense smoke coated the upper reaches in the wafts below the dangling tapestries.

It was mid-afternoon, so the light was beginning to show signs of shifting into dim, almost the same quality of light as after a summer storm that flashed and fled in moments on a bright day.

It was also not busy, and small wonder. With the palace having been so recently violated, no doubt every single on-call soldier, guard and flunky was being kept well within the walls of the Emperor's line of sight. There wouldn't be much business here this week, save for some regular high-merchant patrons or visiting fools.

The girls could not approach. Only a girl who was summoned in some clear verbal or visual manner could approach a customer. But until then, anyone who wanted his patronage could make herself as pleasing at a distance as was possible.

One girl, a buxom variety with crimson lips the shade of almost wounded plums, eyed him with special hunger. Those lips were frequently pursed at the stem of a hookah, which she shared with another girl.

When she passed the stem to the other and exhaled her fragrant smoke, she could skillfully control and shape their release so as to not only give the appearance almost of a woven bead-veil before her face and dissipating just as it reached those kohl-circled eyes (a very small but interesting *magique*, something his father had called a "parlor trick"), but also to let her lips show their fullness and dexterity to maximum effect. Her face was the inverted teardrop of a pearl set in a tiara, but her skin was the dusky color of buffed heartwood, amber in the light. Hair fell in a straight forked waterfall of midnight, barely even shining except where she had jeweled pins holding the hair in the back up in an elaborate coif.

She returned his stare as unblinking as he, and he read her features carefully. Under her shift of gauze silk, forms very pleasant and healthy, available for all manner of promised distractions, rose and fell with each breath. Her turns with the hookah stem and plumes of smoke interrupted the shared gaze at times, but he used those moments to try and take in the whole of her.

Experienced. Not quite as young as some of the others. Nowhere near as naïve.

His eyes broke to sweep back left, then right. Making another assessment of the atrium's offerings.

Willowy things. Most of the girls were the petite-built things of local stock. City girls with no way to move out to any estates unless some rich patron came along and fancied them more than his one pocketbook's holdings. Black hair that was oiled, perfumed, teased into ringlets. One had hers bobbed in a short cut like a *kitsune* demon in old drawings when taking human rather than fox form. There were gigglers and sullen pouters, each trying their variety of enticement. Another was clearly wearing a wig to give her a shimmering curtain of copper tresses, and had applied some powder to her face so she was as dead-white as a *seu-seu*, a conjure-lover in adult fairytales.

Only the girl with the *màgique* for smoke veils and a hot coal to her glower at him seemed of any real solidity. And the longer he thought on it, the more he considered that time was getting away from him and this entire contract was nothing if not an issue of time.

Her, then. She seems one who might even occasionally enjoy the game with the guards, the men who think themselves the masters.

He flicked a hand in beckoning. She didn't give any triumphant smirk or make any remark to any of the others as she set aside the hookah stem and rose from her cushions. The somnolent buzz of bees was the only sound as she came around the pool's circumference to sit beside him. Her expression remained the same glacial regard, her eye contact never breaking.

Careful skills. Well composed. And that mechanical clock behind her eyes, as father described. But very, very well hidden. A thiefkiller and a courtesan. Are we such similar creatures in the Empire, then?

A poet whose poems—

He managed to snap shut the inner box of his thought on that. What Brooms had called the rear-thoughts (so named because to focus on them and not the moment at hand was likely to get you stabbed in that same posterior place).

"And you would be the gentleman...?"

"Fifth Rear Envoy Chrysalis. From the Nippo-Tau Province Collective." Such usefulness as years of reading the Imperial atlases rendered, to be able on the spot to think of a far enough locale and position.

"A far distance you've come. It explains your hair."

"My hair?"

"You tie it back, but no oils or curls like they do in the uncultured suburbs. And no coin-locks hanging behind an ear like the current city fashion dictates. Is it long?"

In answer, he reached up and carefully tugged free a thin lock for her, letting it dangle to his shoulder.

She reached a finger out, the nail pail coral against her skin. Stroked the underside of the lock, starting halfway its length and following it down. She didn't remove her fingertip without letting the back of it, the nail faintly rasping, run along the fabric of his shoulder in a definite motion of negotiation.

"Yet clean and neatly kept," she sighed. "As are those expensively made clothes tailored to be cheap."

"You have a good eye."

"Is Nippo-Tau a prosperous corner of the Empire?"

Another tactic. Gauge if the customer is truly carrying currency worth the trouble, or if they have merely bought a slightly better cut of clothes to appear as more for the one dalliance. He used a similar thinking when he assessed if others were in disguise when he was about to kill, if someone was playing more helpless than they were to draw an assassin too close to stop in time.

"It has its riches and its difficulties, as any other lands have. We're particularly revered for the jeweled pots and woven-rush curtains that are soft as the finest silks after proper dyeing and beating. But I'm only here on a tax collections assay. My supervisor, Second Minister Pond Bottom, said since I was the newest appointment to the offices and this was my first business journey that I should take today to 'see some of the city' to better enrich my knowledge."

Boring but enough to establish a realistic presentation as someone with money but not too much. Another silly bureaucrat from a not-quite-backwater.

"A bit long-of-years for only being someone of Chrysalis at a Fifth Envoy?"

"I was a slow riser from academy."

"Or perhaps you behaved in your youth in ways that weren't considered altogether proper?" She still had not smiled, but there was something of a grin in the way her eyelids dropped at the asking.

He gave a noncommittal shrug. "Perhaps."

"And perhaps you wish to re-live some of those behaviors?" The coral fingertip touched lightly on the cuff of his sleeve. It ran a lazy circle around the carved decorative bone button on the cuff, tracing out the shape of the tailor's trademark etched there. "We may go into the back and see how young a boy I can make you feel, if the price is right."

He dropped his voice to a lower whisper. "Perhaps...I sought out a different type of discretion from you?"

She said nothing. Only stared. But the fingertip held still, no longer lazily tracing buttons.

"That is to say...if you would be compensated for introducing me to a member of the local...special constabulary?"

Still nothing. The slightest tickle of apprehension and doubt started at the hackles of his neck, but he remained calm.

Instead, he went quiet. Finally she gave a faintly theatrical sigh and lay back against the sedan chair's padding back.

"Intrigue is so much more boring than a bit of indiscretion."

"But can be more profitable."

"My head is worth more to me than my purse."

"I assure you neither would be in any danger. I am asking you to do nothing more than perhaps...share you worldly knowledge with a humble envoy who wishes to inquire about some matters of state. Nothing iniquitous."

"The things that are not iniquitous are quite often the worst things entirely."

"Can you be of assistance in this or not?"

"Hrm. I suppose. If we could negotiate a proper compensation for the bother."

"Absolutely. I would expect nothing less."

"Normally, all business is left outside the doors," she faintly flapped a hand at the rattan screen in front of them, in the direction of the half-moon doors to the interior. "But this business is much as intimate as any I had first in mind. So for absolute privacy for these talks, we should adjourn there."

Pon-Chai nodded wordlessly. He allowed her to take his hand and lead him around the screen and past the doors.

Deep within the real heart of the Red Chambers, they discussed matters for the next two and a half hours that further cemented his thoughts of poetry, murder and lust all being of very similar calibers.

When he left, he had the name of a rather lesser-known eatery in the canals district, and a very late hour set to meet someone in the auxiliary guard who was on-alert but not locked up in service to the palace at present.

The courtesan's treachery was pointless, and no longer germane to his contract.

Don't ever go for revenge. Revenge is like stabbing yourself in the foot *trying to remind yourself to kick someone* else *in the* head. *You might achieve it, but you'll pay into an empty contract with yourself to finish. And revenge isn't* professional. *It makes you* stupid. *And stupid men don't become* old *men with us. Leave the things that didn't kill you behind. Unless they can chase after you and try again. Then leave them dead.*

"Yes, sir," he whispered into the empty room.

The courtesan. Leave her and her conniving behind. Inside his mind, where he kept a mental mirror of himself for occasional referencing in the dark or in a rush of disguising himself, he allowed a smirk that never reached his lips.

If he survived, the thought closed its own ribboned loop neatly, *the serious one will no doubt find the time and motivation to go and have words with her at his own leisure. And settle both our accounts for us. Or not. It doesn't matter.*

And another lesson came up from the mind's dark archives: *Don't discount* anyone *as a threat. Man, woman...I've seen a child barely taller than my withered thigh smile at me as it slit a sleeping man's throat in his tent. It doesn't take a man's hand to tip the poison into your drink, or poke your throat with the finest of knives.*

Don't discount anyone.

Unbidden, the image of the beggar-mother snapped up like an unfurled sail catching a harsh side-wind. He used a hand of resolve to try and shove it aside.

She wasn't a killer or threat. She was exactly what she looked like. A beggar pregnant with a nameless child.

The image of her, the sound of her voice pleading, wouldn't be shoved out of sight. It hung behind his eyes, almost as clear as if he were back in that alley.

Keep it there, then. *Something in the back of my mind obviously sees some useless sentimental value in—*

Don't discount anyone.

A pregnant woman.

Have you seen a doctor?

His eyes snapped open.

"Physicians. Chirurgeons. *Thaumagris* and their apprentices..." his voice carried no further than the walls, dying out to the muffled thumps and cries elsewhere. "...oh but there would be the necessary midwives, wouldn't there? Of course there would be."

Now the beggar-mother's image went dark, her voice went quiet and the thought of her was neatly rolled and return to some shelf of scrolls back in his rear-thoughts.

He uncurled his legs, let his feet find the floor, his toes feel bloodflow fully again and sense the wrappings of his shoes, the pants legs around his calves and thighs. His hands remained on his knees as he stared at the smeared and waterstained wall in front of him.

A royal Heir Emperor was nameless until birth. No name-intended could actually be attached to a life until that life emerged into the proper world and was no longer bound by its birth-cord to the mother's name. Having the name would be useless for another couple of months at least, if the recent Imperial Proclamations in the newspapers had been correct. The name was still a crucial treasure, that hadn't changed. But it reminded him that the child was yet unborn.

And a child yet unborn required great attention and care to its progress, by the royal house's best physicians and *m'agique* healers. Indeed. To make sure the mother was eating right, sleeping enough. Getting the fresh air in just the right proportions each day, or staying in when the rain or the city smogs were too dense. All energy of the universe to a baby flowed first through the channel of the mother's rivers. Dieticians, doctors of every examining stripe...

...but physicians were often men, at least in the royal chauvinism that was still held in a sort of ancestral and eldritch awe. Most of the practitioners of the Empress Concubine would be men.

But by that same possessive body of old laws and rules, no other men could touch the flesh of the woman carrying the Heir Emperor. Not even to administer her necessary care or to examine her closely for signs of danger to the unborn.

For that, midwives of some skill had to attend. Women chosen for their cleverness and dexterity to carry out the commands of a physician while at the same time gently tending by touch and careful attention to the patient herself. Hands venturing where no man's other than the Heaven's Own dared to place fingertips even in the most clinical of arrangement.

No. Surely not. All such surgeons and examiners and their assistants are even now under lock and key while the palace continues fruitless investigation.

True. But...

...but...but...the lesser aides are almost always *Untaught. Local midwives picked for skill and attention but not for any formal teaching in the literary arts. For just such a purpose. Isn't it* possible *that these Untaught may be just low enough to escape the palace's consideration as a threat? What Untaught would try and take a name that they couldn't read or comprehend? How would an Untaught even know if it was the proper name they were taking away with them, if they couldn't read it to be sure?*

Yes. An Untaught midwife from the palace retinue. It was possible...it was really the only possibility he could consider still left, when all others were eliminated.

There were a few ways he could use this, to check and be sure. There were a few market options, a place or two he could change tactics and ask his questions to be certain.

His clothes changed and belongings transferred, he blew out the cheap candles that had been left for him by the hotelier. When he closed the door behind him, all he left behind in the room was the ghost of his breaths and the faintest hint of his body warmth. These quickly enough were gone into the cacophony of thumps, cries and arguments that seemed to wallpaper the place.

It was a matter of triangulation. He followed this as he followed Brooms' other teachings thoroughly.

It takes three people minimum to make a plot. One person can just make a mistake, get caught. Two people can fool each other into thinking they're both clever, ready to betray each other to profit as one. But three people invest in something if it is successful at all.

Can't three or more betray as easily as two, sir?

Certainly. But first they must succeed in the plot to have something worth betraying for. Always three. More than that there may be, but there are still only three people at the heart of any entwined act.

Pon-Chai the young man, sitting in front of Three Brooms, the master thiefkiller turned teacher. They were underneath the peach tree in Brooms' courtyard, the one that had an elliptical rut in the dirt beneath its boughs. The rut was the shape of Brooms' voice, the circular turn of his steps as he grumblingly limped back and forth while giving out his lessons.

The veteran would never glance at Pon-Chai to see if he was bored or paying attention. If the young man didn't, his money still spent the same and the young fool would find out his first time attempting a contract that he should have listened.

The best teacher has no stake in a student's failure, and everything in their triumph. Another of his father's lesser sayings.

The first is the Thinker. Brooms was no poet, and Pon-Chai appreciated perhaps most of all the man's rather plain way of describing the concepts he conveyed. *The one that sits in their room and watches clouds, biding time for some moment's chance to get ahead, get some gold to their worthless name. They are the one that must be behind the whole thing. It could be a moment's opportunity, a window that suddenly snaps its curtains aside in a hard wind and reveals to them an opening they can exploit. But the Thinker is smart enough to not only see the open window for what it is, but knows to remember if he's many floors up before jumping. And he will make sure there is a ladder below.*

The Ladder *is the* bridge. *The Thinker wants a step of removal from their risk. So they'll operate through someone who can bridge that distance. And like any good ladder...someone who can be simply knocked away from the window and shoved to fall into the shadow of the bushes below, if the Thinker senses things have gone wrong.*

The Ladder also is a good incrimination. If someone comes along and happens to see the Ladder, they won't necessarily assume it's the Thinker orchestrating anything. Especially if the Thinker is good enough to cry indignity and give sound explanations and alibis. After all, a ladder down *from a window can easily be a ladder* up *to a window as well. The Thinker can often point to the Ladder and cry foul for themselves, make themselves the seeming victim of some act. All to throw the shadows in another direction.*

Pon-Chai swallowed. The taste of the lunch-time wine he'd been permitted to sip was sour at the back of his throat as the teacher struck the far end of his orbit and spun on his limping leg like it was a wooden prosthetic, almost a graceful and thoughtless dance step to spin, pirouette on that foot and then stamp down, regain his step and begin to move past the trunk of the peach tree once more. He smirked and gnawed his lower lip while he parsed out his thoughts to the student.

The last person is the Lookout, *or even the* Steady. *The person at the bottom waiting for the Thinker to climb down. The person who may even be steadying and securing the Ladder, making sure the plan even has any chance of being pulled off. The Steady has to keep an eye out constantly for being caught, being watched, being suspected, even being looked askance at. The Steady is the only one who can be out there at the far end of the plan. But they're also, for all their importance, usually the one who can't rely on getting any fair share of the spoils. They're the ones that will lose their head no matter who else is caught.*

They're the ones all the way out there, like a worm on the dangled end of a hobby-fisher's line, all the time shaking and fearful of being caught, being cut off. If the Thinker kicks the Ladder off, the Steady knows it'll fall right on top of him in the act. The Steady is the one who makes everything happen, but they have the worst chances of losing.

You put them together...the Thinker, the Ladder, the Steady...and you have a plot. You have something that the Thinker, if all goes according to plan, can come out that window, climb down, and be assured of safe passage away and out into the world of their dream. With minimal to no investment in the Ladder or the Steady being any better off once they have served their use.

Pon-Chai watched the old killer reach the far left end of the ellipse and spin, but this time he stopped to look down at his pupil.

So...tell me then: how do you deal with such a plot? Who do you find?

Pon-Chai, his hair not yet as long as to cover his smallish ears, had grimaced into his own lap for a long minute. Then he returned his master's gaze.

It would make no sense to go after the Thinker. He already has at least two removes between him and any one else. And deniability.

Good. Go on.

And the Ladder is just a ladder. Someone could easily move on to some other window, some other opportunity, or the Thinker could, as you said, kick them away and let them fall unused to the ground.

You may have the grasp of it. Three Brooms nodded, giving no indication if he was happy or bemused with this train of answer, only encouraging that more of it come.

*But...*here Pon-Chai's grimace returned...*but to go after the Steady would be pointless as well. As you say, they make the plan possible, but they are also the easiest to catch. The ones who have the least value to the threatening of the plan, only its success. If they fail, it is possible others could be found to replace them without disturbing the Ladder or the Thinker.*

An interesting problem, then, isn't it?

Pon-Chai nodded. Then: *Wait...*

Yes?

You asked me one question...but that is not the only *question, is it?*

Now his master gave the weakest look of a grin at the corners of his heavy-lipped mouth. He scratched at his sheep's wool head of iron curls and nodded. *Go on.*

It is not just who *you must go find. It is* when *you must find them. When in the course of their plot when they are all the most vulnerable. Then you have the best chance of affecting the plot, or finding those involved.*

Very good. Three Brooms stepped over to the peach tree and thumped into a lean against it. A few blossoms fluttered to the ground. Pon-Chai's eye automatically tracked the movement of the petals.

You aren't finished, Brooms prompted him. *Keep moving with it. You have a grab on the ribbon, now keep pulling at it, see the whole thing through.*

The petals reached the dirt of Brooms' pacing rut in the ground.

Movement. From tree to ground. Down...but it wasn't while on the branch or on the ground that the wind could move it the most...

When the Thinker thinks it's safe. When he begins to climb down the Ladder to the ground. He is already committed to the plot at last. The Ladder must be there to see it through as well. The Steady may run, but they are the least important at that point, and anyway they will most likely stay and await the Thinker safely down, hoping for their reward.

Three Brooms glanced up into the leaves and fragrant buds of the peach tree.

This is my grave tree. Have I told you that?

Pon-Chai shook his head.

Brooms reached one large, delicate-fingered hand up, over his head, back and patting at the bark of the tree trunk. *This is where I've done much of my best thinking. And it's pleasant. I've earned being buried in a place far from anyone I've put down being raised against me.*

It's a beautiful tree, Pon-Chai offered lamely. This wasn't a conversation he comprehended, but stayed attentive.

Brooms peered at the writer's son. *Your parents paid a pretty price to give you a special name.*

The young man sucked in a breath. *How—*

Oh be quiet a moment now. Even Recorder Generals are able to be broken, or worked around, if one is smart and careful and patient enough. I don't know your virtuous name, boy. But all I had to do was make a very general statement like that and you practically told it to me with your reaction, didn't you?

Pon-Chai recomposed himself. *I'm sorry, sir.*

No, it's all right. Names are given too much weight. Your school teacher probably taught you as soon as you had your mouth off your mother's breast all about m'agique *threats and virtuous names versus all the other layers of names and artifice every person of position has to maintain to keep some alley-cat tabulamancer from taking over their brain or cursing their livestock with a whisper of their virtuous, oh-so-fancy-and-unique true name.*

But aren't those things true?

Yes. But all that only matters if you are a person who still cares about anyone else knowing who you really are.

The mentor hunched down, his back still against the trunk, level with Pon-Chai.

A killer can't afford that. People's names have lessening power over them as they create new social-names and false-names because they don't actually value those things much, if at all. Do you see the mechanism I'm speaking of?

I...believe I do.

That name—whatever it is—is only as truly important as you choose it to be for you. And you can only be hurt by others as much as you stupidly allow them to be capable of doing it. I have studied with some of the best in cardsharps and confidence men in the busiest of criminal provinces, learning the ways to hide intent and control response...and do you know the rule that every one of them agrees is as universal as gravity and sunlight?

No.

'You cannot ever cheat a truly honest person.'

Now the old man lowered himself completely to the soil, his bad leg straightening out from under him. Wincing, he rubbed fingers into the tendons and injured muscles of his knee and calf.

You cannot truly cheat someone who never cheats. You cannot hurt someone if they first do not put themselves in a place where their throat is bared to your hands. The same must be true for you if you mean to really follow me down this fool's road of a life. And your name, your special virtuous name that everyone thinks will kill you with a glance if the wrong wizard gets wind of it...it can only be as vulnerable as you leave it.

Done massaging his injured limb, he criss-crossed his fingers together and rested them on his small curve of belly.

My mother was brought here from another country. A land called 'Kay-Frica.' The mother continent, some heathens believe it. When she arrived here, the first thing my father did was make sure that he paid good gold for a proper name for his son-to-be. He was a robber baron, but his gold was as shiny as anyone else's to the Record General's offices. But being the man he was, he wasn't rich or spendthrift enough to buy me a truly good name. Just a little-used and therefore expensive one. He bought me a virtuous name that hasn't been used in at least three thousand years, and probably will one day be gone from any written record as the papers fade and the papyri mold and moth-ball.

Or would, if I hadn't already stolen its record from those same vaults years ago.

Pon-Chai made no movement or sound. He knew that shocking things were now meant to prod and see if he weakened in his lessons.

Three Brooms nodded, but in approval or punctuation of his story it was unclear.

I took back my name, and my father and mother were lost to sea on one of his jaunts in that stupid junk of his when I was barely knee-high. So no one knows my name but me, and I have never given it to anyone. And never will.

Not even to a truly beloved? But Pon-Chai knew not to ask. Three Brooms would not laugh at the prospect, but it would be far worse if he seemed saddened or disappointed at the student even mentioning the concept. Thiefkillers could not have a truly beloved. Love was as much a thief as any beggar-boy with a hand in your tunic. And the professional's life killed it dead as any other assassin.

When I die, and this peach sheds its blossoms as the only tears that'll ever be shed for my passing, my name will die with me. No other child will be given it, and no jack-dime m'agique *slinger will ever be able to raise me and interrupt my sleep to run about as some idiot* wight *or ghoul-stepper.*

Three Brooms tucked his bad leg in against his stomach, not quite achieving the three-points form as Pon-Chai more easily could with his undamaged legs.

If you insist on valuing something, valuing yourself, but you don't take the proper steps to ensure its security. If you don't truly care enough to make it as safe as you can from anyone else hurting you, then don't whine in the afterlife about your murderers. You're your own killer. *You're just mad that someone else was holding the knife even though you bared the throat.*

Pon-Chai thought about these things for a time. Finally he gave a single tilt of his head. *Thank you.*

No thanks needed. You paid for that homily as much as any others I've spouted off the last three months. And you'll no doubt get more than your money's worth before we're done.

Another reach of the hand up to pat the tree trunk.

Only this tree might mourn me, and then only until someone else comes along to water it.

The old man looked at him with eyes sharper than the tip of a night-arrow, held to the shaft of a taut oiled crossbow.

But I think...you at least *are something I will leave behind. I thought that I would take everything with me before you came and tricked me into teaching you. Even my virtuous name. The way you saw the proper question, and its answer, for something that even I had to have struck upside my head to learn...I think I will be fine if you are the only thing I leave behind as any sign that I was ever here in this world.*

Pon-Chai only gave another tilt of his head. But inside, he thought there was a whirlwind scattering the peach blossom petals of his thoughts.

*

Triangulation.

The Thinker, the Ladder, the Steady.

Find the members. Never mind the Thinker...they probably weren't even in the city.

But the Ladder might be within reach...and the Steady would be on the run, attempting to get away safely so as to remain a part of the plot and hoping for reward.

The canals and ports would be under constant auxiliary patrols to prevent anyone leaving by those means. But anyone with feet could get out of the city by any one of untold numbers of ways.

The public gates were under guard and searching all outgoing or incoming travelers. Only merchants with special vetting and dispensation papers were allowed leave. All incoming merchants were charged higher sales tariffs as the cost of doing business for arriving in the palace city at such a bad time.

Pon-Chai walked to the eastern districts of the city, along the line of the fortress walls that buttressed the buildings along that border. It took him the better part of the day to cover the distance, but he didn't want to hire a wagon or rickshaw, and didn't trust horses in the traffic and noise.

He stopped once in a side-market to purchase some peaches and a pirate-lime. They were not quite in-season, and tasted a bit bitter being not-fully-ripened. But he was grateful for the tartness, and they still bore plenty of refreshing juice. It was eating one of the peaches while he walked that had him thinking of Three Brooms and his grave tree in the courtyard.

And yet I had to burn down the house in the end, he considered while spitting out the pit after he'd thoroughly chewed any lingering meat off it. *And no doubt that peach tree and all else in the courtyard burned with it. Did I destroy the old man's last legacy of value?*

But he knew the answer to that was the answer to everything else. Three Brooms had bought his home for comfort and distance, much as Pon-Chai had had his built and his estate out in the suburban lands for him and his mother. But he had had no sentiment attached to anything. Every sentiment was another ribbon tied to his deepest heart, and as he'd made clear to his pupil that day under the tree, he'd long before made certain that even his own name could not be held against him as a knife to his veins.

After all, he greeted me with a knife to my belly when I first came to him. Pon-Chai grinned as he pulled the pirate-lime out of his pocket, beginning with a deft fingernail to peel the thin rind off the pungent, handball-sized citrus. *And when we parted, it was the same way. Just to prove there was no nostalgia for my company when I left.*

The pirate-lime, removed of its emerald wrapping, was mostly a giant pit-seed, a stone-hard thing that would crack teeth before it cracked itself. But popping it into his mouth and rolling it back and forth, squirreling it from cheek to cheek, it had a vigorous flavor rich with acid that he knew was good for his health. It would keep his energy up and helped guard against infections in the pits of the cities. Sailors took barrels of them as an easy way to keep their health on long voyages, and he'd borrowed the trivia as he'd collected so many other things in his rear-thoughts over the years. Some useful, others merely the pleasure of collecting and knowing, perhaps sharing with his mother when he was home.

Market stalls, barkers calling out to come and see strange wonders imported from other lands. The smells of animals and perfumes, incense and old fruit. Fresh-cut meat and fish resting atop blocks of ice brought out from the winter cellars of storehouses. The sounds of people calling out to each other. The sight of old friends finding each other in front of a café, hugging and clapping hands to backs in their discovery.

Pon-Chai took everything in, and nearly all of it passed through him much as any sigh through a hollow tube. There was nothing here to catch him, only delay him if he allowed it to distract.

But when he arrived at the eastern neighborhoods he slowed and began to observe things more carefully. In a public fountain he washed his hands and face, listening to the talk of washer-women collecting buckets, the children lingering about them. The girls preparing to meet a suitor. Young merchant apprentices who were frustrated in their dead-end positions and returning from an abbreviated lunch.

Bits and pieces. Like shriveled peppers on a string, bits and pieces that needed proper reading to tell which could be used and which were meaningless.

He drank coffee at a table of an outdoor café near the fountain, in a place where much of the moving traffic from the next neighborhood entered into the bloodflow of those coming in from the largest eastern gates.

"Damned tariff! Might as well have turned and gone back home for all the profit it'll leave us! And the leaving you know they'll take their full share of the sales as well!"

A pair of donkeys pulling a cart laden with spicewood in its raw cut logs. A smell of something like cedar burning in a soup of cimmamon and a heartwood that glowed like clean oak when buffed, spicewood was handy for making sturdy, inexpensive furnishings that looked far richer under layers of varnish than they cost to make. Spicewood only grew in a handful of far districts and nowhere near the city. The merchant leading his animals and complaining to his apprentice didn't seem to care if anyone overheard his gripes.

"It's fine," the apprentice said. "We can arrange to leave with our profit intact. We'll just pay Sao-Ke and—"

A smack of a hand against the apprentice's shoulder silenced him. "Idiot! Keep your mouth shut about that!"

That was a start.

Leaving the café. More listening. Someone else spoke no names but talked quietly in a smoke-tavern about paying a 'lesser tax' to get out of the city around the guard. Another person muttered about Sao-Ke in another coffeehouse.

It was twilight by the time he caught enough of the spiders that their silk wove into anything like a canvas he could then paint a plan upon with the most delicate of brushes.

Sao-Ke was a Guild Tender, or to some a slightly grander version of a Tomcat Prince in the eastern neighborhoods. He oversaw the handling of illicit activities ostensibly without being under the auspices of any Empire oversight. The working reality as Pon-Chai pieced together was that the Emperor and his offices could quite easily stomp down on any size operation that dealt in various criminalities; but it was deemed wiser to let the more brutal and intelligent leaders emerge from the beatings and competitions and thus keep a certain harmony even amongst the cutthroats and unlicensed prostitutes. Give them some leash, and the dogs would think themselves free...to a controllable point. If chaos could seep into all things as groundwater into a root cellar, Guild Tenders and their like were the rudest of shelves to keep the potatoes and spices off the ground and out of the flooding. Not perfect, but cheap and the simplest way to keep things at bay. They knew their place and their size, and truces and parley tracts were maintained amongst the shifting districts.

Sao-Ke apparently had means by which to secret the right persons who paid the proper costs out of the city. Without the guards and patrols catching wind of it. According to the proper district record rules, he was noted publicly as Eastern Gray Stork. Sao-Ke was the under-public slang name for him, but everyone knew who you spoke of if you inquired (carefully) about 'being delivered by the Stork.'

Eastern Gray Stork was supposed to be most frequently found at one of his properties: a cookhouse that specialized in beef dishes and discreet booths for large meetings. It was nearly midnight before Pon-Chai found himself at the entrance, a place painted in subdued dark woodstains and with no banners or bright tapestries advertising its exterior. A hot smell of fresh meat cooking in braziers greeting him as he entered.

He paid a small fee to the man keeping to the tea table, buying a cup of cheap peach-and-honey tea (was that, too, as constant in this city as babies and crying in the night?). He took a seat at a small table where he could see the large rear-wall dining booths...very reminiscent of the smaller negotiation alcoves at Red Chambers but for their round tables with the serving spinners mounted in the centers, and muttering parties of a half-dozen or more discussing politics and local business.

It wasn't hard to see which table had to be the Stork's. It was the one that only had a single man sitting at it, and no screens in front of it so he had an unobstructed view of the room about him. He was ignoring a bowl of dark soup and writing on a small pad of paper.

No. He's not alone. Only the table is alone. Look and see.

Of course. The tea table had another patron sitting there but that man never seemed to finish his tea, just swirled the cup about and inhaled the cooling fragrance. The man who had sold him his cup, too, seemed to be staying at this end of the table countertop, wiping and wiping and wiping with a small rag as if there were some unseen but irremovable stain there to be fought with.

If anyone tried to approach Stork at his table, no doubt at least one or all of these men would very swiftly and definitely put themselves between that person and the table. If someone decided to make an issue of being obstructed, no doubt more individuals would come forth and that someone would be fast removed...and if fortunate only evicted from the building.

But now it was too much, too long finding one person and wasted time into another thread. So he got up and took his emptied cup to the tea counter.

"More?" The man tipped the steaming pot towards his cup, eyebrows raised.

Pon-Chai shook his head. "Thank you, but I would prefer to meet with the Stork and discuss some business, if you or your compatriot here would be willing to make the proper introductions for me." He nodded back at the table he had been sitting at. "I'll wait there until he's ready."

He didn't make it back to his seat before the voice called out. "Hold." He turned to see the man at the private table was no longer writing at his papers. He was staring directly at Pon-Chai, his pen put down.

Almost as if there had been a royal proclamation, the rest of the room's whispers and hushes died away further. People at other tables tried to pretend they weren't looking out of the corners of their eyes at what was happening.

"What business would you have in the east streets? You clearly are no *citiman*. A *citiman* would have had more sense."

Some soft, sycophant snickers amidst other tables. An archaic insult, something yet again borrowed from another land and time, suggesting he was stupider than some toadying urban bureaucrat.

"Would you like me to talk the details aloud across the room, or may I join you for a more private discussion?" Pon-Chai made a pointed glance to the tea counter. "I'm unfamiliar with all the customs of the palace city. Is it normal to conduct all one's clandestine business out in the middle of a crowded restaurant?"

The man looked back at Pon-Chai. He gave a nod to the man at the counter, who jerked his head in the direction of the table to Pon-Chai.

Pon-Chai slowly and with as few deliberate, slow and openly-visible movements as he could, took the seat opposite the Stork, his back to the open room just as undoubtedly intended. His entire back felt very cold as he took the seat, but knew not to look over either shoulder. He would have to either trust the professional integrity of this Stork, or not at all and then it was pointless to be here.

The Stork was not some stereotypical fatuous, gluttonous overlord sitting fat in his overpadded chair. He was a large-eyed, scarecrow-built man. Whip-thin and wearing what was called a 'battery' hat, a sort of cylindrical hat of rich black velvet that sat on his head, one tassel hanging to the side of his head, a ruby accent jewel winking in the candlelight of the table's centerpiece from the swinging fringe. His robes were also black silk of the finest quality, simply but more than competently cut and stitched so neatly he almost seemed to wearly a form-fitting swatch of shadow. The buttons were forced pearl, black but shining.

The handwriting Pon-Chai saw on the papers before him was slanted but consistent, neat. The writing of a schooled man, raised somewhere other than the dirtier back street districts. His face had the curves and gaunt sunken places of a mummy, but his skin was youth-smooth and only a pair of slight sleepless bags under his blinking heartwood eyes gave any indication he was any older than Pon-Chai.

He sat back against the booth seat, taking in Pon-Chai. Finally, his voice gave a measured chuckle.

"I think you gave Bagger his first surprise in eight years, since his wife tried to kill him."

"Bagger?"

"The tea man."

"Considering the quality of the brew he gave me, I am surprised it's been so long since someone tried again."

The Stork gave another slow blink. Twice. Then smiled.

"Not a *citiman*, but you managed to find this place and make it to my table. So perhaps not as foolish as first perceived."

"I welcome someone seeing me as a fool. So much the easier to hide, then."

The Stork blinked.

Then he took a slow, considering sip of his soup.

The golden spoon clinked against the fine porcelain of the bowl, filigreed around the wide rim with accents of mother-of-pearl. It was not the kind of dishware anyone else in the establishment enjoyed.

He put the spoon down. Swallowed the soup with some savoring on his face.

"You are not a citiman. Not a common merchant or tradesman."

"I am a tradesman, though not of any business you might find useful."

"What is your business, then? And may I have your name?"

"I am a wandering poet. I came to the city to try my latest verses on the people and gauge their response. You may call me Lowly Squid."

"Lowly Squid?"

"I have yet to feel worthy of even the ink I have wasted writing my words."

The Stork blinked. "There is a flattering honesty in that last statement."

This was not the smiler or even his almost-aware serious companion in a dirty canal eatery. This was a truly serious man...a grave one. And a man who did not hold the knife out for you to see, but gave the nod to the ones in the darkness who did.

The handwriting. The fine clothes that were cheaply designed but expensively commissioned. The battery hat, which was favored amongst certain intelligentsia who believed it helped keep the head warm and thus preserved brain function the best. The Stork was not someone he could play with or banter too long against. Best to move to his purpose. This was dancing where neither partner could lead, but neither could misstep.

"How have your verses fared so far?"

"Passing fair. I had a masterpiece I had hoped would work out, but my pride played me false on its quality. It ended up being a whole falsehood of bad prose."

"Such is any thing we think of as great ourselves, in our works." The Stork sighed, taking another sip from his soup. He did not offer anything to Pon-Chai, and no servants brought any cups or asked anything of the men at the table. The murmurs of the room had gone back to their original volume, but in a decidedly guarded manner.

"But while here, I nevertheless found inspiration amongst the city folk to try a new line of poetry. And I have heard that you might be able to help me research some of its lore so I can put down the lines just right."

"I'm not a great one for poetry. Or folklore." The candle flame barely puffed on its wick from their words. The light was steady and glistened off the buttons the same as it did off the Stork's wet-blinking eyes. "It may be that for your cleverness you have nonetheless come to the wrong house to ask."

"I was told that Sao-Ke was an ingenious man, a Guild Tender of the first and highest mark. Perhaps it was only folklore, indeed, that I heard people mutter about at the fountains and abattoir doors."

The Stork did not blink. Stared at Pon-Chai and betrayed one flick of his eyes beyond him, to the men at the tea table. Pon-Chai continued.

"The city towers are quite keen and watching, more than I would have thought any average day warranted without some alarm or alert of a criminal being sought on great dangers or treasons. The city gates, too, are quite enamored of closing shut and reopening on every other traveler seeking entrance or exit. Many questions are being asked, few answers being traded. Yet no one speaks of any calamity."

The Stork took another calm sip of soup.

"But this still has made so many nervous, eager to fly and migrate back to their snowy hills or sunny islands, what coins they may earn enough to satisfy them. But not, as others have overhead, quite enough to make it worth paying the sales tax tolls to be allowed to leave by the orthodox venues."

Now the Guild Tender nodded. "I have tried to listen as any wise man would. All anyone can hear is a lot of fishwife talk and old fool speculations. The palace is locked down, the auxiliary called off leave, and no one of any government office is permitted to leave the city by any means, until such a time as to be indefinitely determined. I have heard everything from the Emperor was eaten by a swarm of fiery snakes before his whole court, to the Royal Concubine was caught by a palace guard making love to her favorite handmaiden in the Lesser Garden of Gray Morning. All of it idiocy."

"And yet the gates slam and swing with the frequency of birds, unsettled at the scent of a cat lurking near. And yet the guards are all armored, spears never leaving their hands night and day."

The Stork dipped his spoon, stirred it without raising it to sip. His eyes were down on the bowl but all attention remained on his dining partner. "Indeed. But in the greater scheme of things, what happens within the court matters very little out here."

"Perhaps. But in this case, what has happened within the court may have quite literally walked through these halls and out into the wild. In which case I have heard the only way it would be possible would have been with the help of the mythic Sao-Ke."

"Myths have a way of being a waste of air and promises."

"But as any poet will tell you, it is often these same great people whose fables inspire the real men and women to take hope and do great deeds."

The spoon stopping swirling. The Stork looked back up.

"What do you want?"

"I am looking for two things. The first would be someone who may have come to you or one of your subordinates and paid for unmonitored flight from the city in the last three days."

"And the second thing?"

"For you to facilitate my leaving the same way."

The Stork picked up his pen. Crossed something out, jotted an addendum to the crossed-out line to the side of the margin beside it. He talked as he scribbled.

"Either of those would be an expensive prospect. Together could be even more mythical a possibility than Sao-Ke."

"Expense is not my concern. Timeliness and accuracy is. Would you have heard of such a person?"

"Money alone is not much currency for strangers in the city. There are values of trust and potential risk that must also be negotiated."

"Any man of wealth and position in the city must consider its loss, not just his momentary gain. I understand."

"Do you?" The Stork blinked back at him, the pen frozen in his grip. "Perhaps. Perhaps not. A man from a high-born country hamlet may appreciate some principles of business, but still be wholly ignorant of the unique facets and nuances of operating in the shadow of the palace."

"All shadows are the same color around the world. Only the shapes and angles at which they are cast at the noon hour are different."

"Yet some shadows are shallower than others. It's the ones dark enough a man could get lost in he should consider carefully before simply blundering along, hands outstretched and trusting to find a guiding hand waiting for him. Instead of a hole."

"What a liar you have been, Stork."

The Stork's face went as still as his pen. "Excuse me?"

"And here you said you were not interested in poetry."

The Stork considered his words and smiled. "We may do some small transaction then. But your money is not my utmost consideration. Such things are hardly my main source of revenue."

"What *is* your utmost consideration?"

"Who I am getting my revenue from."

"I thought I had told you."

"Let us say...I am a plain man, underneath my silks." The pen was set down, and now the Stork leaned towards the table, crossing his arms casually on its top as he peered at Pon-Chai. "And I need plainer speaking."

"I have not been successful as a poet, to be fair." Pon-Chai felt the coldness at his back go down another degree. "And so for additional funds, I sometimes have been commissioned to work on others' works. To proof and check for errors, grammar and rhythm balance. I was recently commissioned on a unique contract."

"Which would be?"

"A case of plagiarism."

"A serious charge amongst the literary."

"Yes. Someone has made off with a quite valuable bit of writing, and the fear is that this work may be...copied. Taken credit for by other parties with no right to the claim. I have been asked to seek the thief out and if possible to...confirm that the work taken is indeed a copy of my client's own. And to make sure it is safely dealt with with no...loss of the work's originality."

The Stork blinked. "Supposed I gave the nod to Bagger and his brother there, Sour. And they came over and picked you up by your arms, and took you somewhere where we could talk at greater length and leisure, but at a far greater disadvantage to you than you labor under now? And at the end of our discussion, the quality of your responses would help me determine if you were to merely be drowned in a nearby washing-basin and dumped on some distant university doorstep as a warning to other idiot poets...or slowly slivered like a bag of bloody almonds and fed to various parrots throughout the district to toughen them?"

Pon-Chai brought his hands from his lap to the table, and rested them palms-down on the table, almost as a magician preparing to begin the patter of a card trick.

"I have no reputation with you here. I am not a great patron of the towers and spires here. And I am no colleague of your field from some brother district. I am merely a messenger and courier here. Trying to track down a lost work and return it. I am willing to pay you for your troubles and expenses in extricating me from the city. But there is nothing else beyond some coins I could give you for your...conversational efforts. You and your men would be wasting their time."

"Or perhaps you would find some way to put a few drops of spider-bark in my soup?"

It was Pon-Chai's turn to blink at last.

"The canals are not where I primarily have business interests, being so far on the other end of the city straits from here. And a far uglier place as well. But spider-bark is not a common poison, even here where court intrigues and whore disputes so often lead to wives putting funny things in their husband's beer. I got word of it from my assets there. And based on the descriptions I received, I had thought it of no consequence. Yet here you are."

"Here I am."

The Stork gave a bitter smirk and shook his head.

"Not a moment ago, I stupidly and arrogantly made the remark that what affects the court has little ripple to us out here in the greater world. And you more astutely said that such a thing may have indeed walked through my doors. My own dismissal of the story of you and those imbeciles trying to rob you, thinking it curious but of no bother, mere trivia. And here you are. Proving the very point."

Pon-Chai said nothing.

"All right then." The hands uncurled, the right patting gently at the waxed cotton tablecloth. "All right then...I will take as read that you are...a professional man in your right. And will ask nothing more than necessary for the tasks at hand."

"I had heard Sao-Ke was also a great man of etiquette and discretion."

"Spare me." A dismissing sigh. "Sao-Ke is an idiot man who has allowed his name to become too popular. Perhaps this is my sign that it's time for someone to have a word with Sao-Ke in a few corners and see that his legend dies out."

"You know what they say. *Legends are as ink on water. They leave their mark and are quickly dispersed...but the water will never be wholly clean again.*"

"Quite true as verses go," The Stork nodded. "47th Dynasty?"

Stupid! Shut up with the poetry! Pon-Chai only shrugged. "It is something I picked up. I do not know its provenance."

"Sloppy for such a studious poet. But never mind." A hand came up, the black sleeve falling back to reveal a white forearm, hairless and horribly acid scarred on the inside flesh. Then the Stork was waving his hand, beckoning to his man. "I need a fresh bowl. This has gotten settled like mud at the river bottom." When the one called Bagger came near, the faint body heat flexing against the cold at Pon-Chai's back, the Stork ordered fresh soup, and two cups of house best tea. "And bring around a screen," the Stork finished. "Have Sour bring that while you get me the soup. We have some matters to talk. And when you've done that, bring me Mother Blue Spur to arrange the usual."

The arm lowered, the sleeve once again concealing the scars. The Stork made a fast notation at the bottom of the paper and put the pen down again.

"We shall discuss matters of money and cost shortly. And issues of people's comings and goings in the city as well. But not until I've had fresh soup and a palate cleansing of hot mint-glow tea." His gaze steadied. "Perhaps for a small part of your compensation, you trade me a courtesy. One professional to another, and not requiring you to give me another lie about your contract."

Pon-Chai inclined his head. "If I am at liberty to share, it is yours."

The Stork's eyes glittered with a sheen totally unlike the buttons on his blouse as he smiled, now with a more vulpine genuineness that reminded Pon-Chai once again that this was not a backroom bandit.

"I would very much like to hear the particular blend you prepared your spider-park powder with. Call it a trade secret, for my trivial curiosity as a fellow poet."

*

There were more quiet arrangements traded after the screen was placed at the opening of the booth, and fresh soup and hot tea were brought before the two professionals. By the time the woman arrived and took a silent seat to the right of Pon-Chai, spider-bark powder had long since been politely debated against the merits of more-readily available (but more easily detectable by a forensic examiner) poisons.

The Stork extended a hand to the woman. "Mother Blue Spur is a fellow specialized individual, quite talented in her ways. I do not handle every single detail of my businesses. Much as the gods do not bother with every feather ruffling on a bird's chest."

"But she might know if any recent feathers in particular have been ruffled?"

"You can speak to me directly," Mother Blue Spur said with a flat, nasal twang to her vocatives. Not a city woman any more than he was a *citiman*. "I am no one's wife or borrow-mistress."

Pon-Chai nodded. "Apologies. Of course you are not."

She said nothing about accepting or rejecting his attempt at reconciliation. She looked to the Stork. "This is another who wants out?"

"You last reported to me a week ago," the Stork said. "How has trade been in sending pigeons off with their notes?"

"Slower. You know how a city lockdown chokes things in the first days. Took nearly four days for me to get a hold on the auxiliary guard contacts and negotiate the newest bribes. I only started having access the last day."

At this, Pon-Chai sparked. "Only the last day?"

She flicked a look at him. "That's what I said." This woman had hair the color of soiled wheat, and it was pulled back in a severe ponytail so tight that the dome of her head seemed coated in a polished wooden helmet. There were two slender silver needles driven through the crux of her ponytail, and he knew there was no way those were merely decorative hairpins. Her face was blockish, resembling something chopped from a tree trunk and mounted in old village shrines. Not a pleasing face to anyone seeking the sort of powdered gigglers that sighed in places like Red Chambers. She wore a man's cut of trousers and a tightly-cinched charcoal tunic. And despite not carrying any weapons openly, he further doubted that this woman went about without something more substantial hidden on her than two silver needles in her hair.

"This gentleman has engaged your services via my proxy," the Stork soothed, sipping at his latest bowl of soup (he had finished two more while they'd talked). "You may speak to him with the same confidence you would speak to me."

She seemed to think this was a foregone conclusion with or without his permission. But she still turned to Pon-Chai. "It's been even worse than in times of quarantine or during the Thirteen Sow riots. Something has every guard on full alert and my usual contacts were not willing to compromise even when I tripled their prices."

"But I take you you've finally managed to arrange a passage through the guard?"

She nodded. "I had to shift my focus a step or two up from the spear-lobbers. Not my usual territory, but I had a girl or two that I was able to parley to some lonely man-at-arms. It did the work. As do they."

"Have you since then enacted any flights from the city? Of any women?"

Blue Spur made a show of slowly turning back to the Stork. "How do you know this man? Truly?"

"Truly? I don't know him at all." The Stork didn't look up from his soup. "He arrived at my table less than an hour ago. With a deal more courtesy and grace than you have, I would add." A sip of the soup. "Though he *has* given me a very excellent argument for his recipe of spider-bark to better envenom your...hair decorations."

Blue Spur gave an exaggerated groan-hiss as she regarded Pon-Chai afresh. "Do you know her?"

"I know *of* her."

"She paid twice the going rate, which surprised me because not only did she not haggle or negotiate with me over anything, but she looked like she barely had two coppers to rub together, let alone a small purse of silver mint."

Pon-Chai raised an eyebrow. "Silver mint?"

"We value the coin," the Stork replied casually. "Even though it's old money. Silver is silver."

"She wanted out as soon as possible. She sat in two safehouses until I had the opening to move her. She kept her mouth shut after the first meet. Barely ate anything. All in all, one of my least troublesome customers." She gave a bemused flick in his direction, but he didn't rise to any argument. "I guess you want the same service? Whose wife have you gotten pregnant?"

It was half-a-jest. "Why would you say that?"

"The woman was quiet. Didn't speak much at all, mostly yes or shaking her head no. But one thing I could easily gather: she wore a physic's tunic, that annoying cloud blue that stands out a damned mile on a cloudy day. A midwife, or some 'prentice to one. Usually they only are trying to get out of the city when they've angered some rich patron." Her chopped-wood lips twisted. "Made her burn that blue tunic before we moved."

"Did she give any name?"

Blue Spur shook her head. "Nothing. I christened her Little Wife Bent Flute. On account of that lack of a flapping mouth of hers."

"Was there any indication where she intended to go?"

Another shake of the head, silver needles glinting. "Nothing. All she needed was for us to get her safely out of the city and away from the patrols."

"Roughly where would that require you to take her?"

"There is a village, some miles outside the city walls. We have a way out of the city to a safe distance from the tower seers, and from there we have some back roads, old logger paths from back when there were still forests and wood embattlements northeast of the city. The paths allow you to reach the village and from there you're on your own."

"Wouldn't the city patrol overseers be aware of those old paths, if they're as old as you say?"

Blue Spur scratched the significant length of her beak nose with a fingernail flicked quickly in her annoyance. "That's what bribes are for, you fool."

"You can bribe entire patrol squadrons?"

A roll of eyes. "You only need to control an overseer or a sergeant to have the whole patrol routed."

Pon-Chai smiled. "Impressive."

"When do you need to leave here?"

It was already fortune enough that the palace restrictions had delayed his quarry and narrowed the lead down to a little over a day. Best not to ask the fates to give him a second smile.

"As soon as possible."

She thought about it a moment. "If it's only you and no cargo, we could still manage you tonight, before dawn. Assuming you can keep up on a swift move."

"His swiftness of foot is not a problem," the Stork spoke from his soup, smiling while he sipped, jotting something new down on his papers with his other hand. "That I can most certainly attest."

Mother Blue Spur led Pon-Chai swiftly from the restaurant by way of a secreted back door that seemed to open onto a completely blocked-in alley, with red brick walls on all sides and no opening to the sky three stories overhead. He watched silently as she walked to the dead end, a few yards ahead of him and only lit by the light falling over him through the back door of the restaurant. Before the door closed behind them and cut the light off, he saw her reach into a seemingly featureless gravel-strewn length of ground and suddenly pull back a square of wood paneling upon which the gravel had been cleverly affixed to match the surrounding ground.

He gave himself several blinks to let his eyes adjust to the darkness to see her waving him over.

"The ladder's a half-leg down on this inside edge," she hissed. "Try not to break your damn-fool neck."

She followed after him, pulling the panel shut and making a twisting motion that was accompanied with faint clicks.

"Clever trapdoor," he whispered. "But not much good if anyone ever were to raid this place."

"We're not in danger of any raids," she snapped. A crack signaled the flaring of a match to life, which was used to light a small steel lantern swinging from Blue Spur's grip. She held it up to shoulder-height and jerked her head forward. "Follow me and try to not trip on your own damned feet."

The tunnel was narrow. His shoulders would brush it if he didn't slant his walk and hunch. And Pon-Chai was a relatively small-built man for the country of his birth. It was dug earth, supported by crossbeams of petrified wood, gray and ghostly as the lantern light picked each next beam ahead in the gloom. Some dust sifts made playful hissing spirits floating about them as the light came and passed.

The tunnel went downwards sharply the first leg, a good two minutes' shuffling jog. Then it curved to level and there was a definite feel of pressure in the air shifting. Deepening. How far down had they gone, he wouldn't have ventured any guess. Far enough that the city walls overhead didn't instantly crush this small tunnel, beams shoring it or not. Far enough that there wasn't the remotest sound of anything above. No carts over a cobble street, no pounding of feet or soldier patrols going over. The only sounds were the huffing of their breaths and the occasional odd rill-trickle of water from some unseen fissure. The air was moist, cool, nearly dank.

How long had they been traveling? He never wore a wristwatch. Such things were useful, but notoriously needing of constant winding and tending and fussing. More a trinket than a tool. He consulted his inner clock and considered that they'd already been moving down here for the better part of an hour. They met a sharp turn to the right and followed it. There were no branches off the tunnel, it was the one corridor winding along. Another turn a few hundred yards further took them left, only ten yards or so took them left again.

Were they circumventing something above? The foundation or armory cellar of one of the city towers that had Imperial seers constantly using farsight spells to spot anyone trying to escape or infiltrate the capital? The walls of the tunnel never varied, consistently showing the crossbeams at the same intervals, the same clay-clingy packed quality of the dirt. The ground under them was not muddy despite that naggingly constant sound of water; it was packed down so hard by either design or years of traffic as to be sound as concrete.

Another fifty yards forced them to take another right, and he gauged that they'd resumed their original direction.

Everything cool and damp, but no puddles or drips anywhere that he detected. But that strange high-pitched, almost plaintive drip-trickle of water...

"Are we underneath the buried aqueducts of the First City?"

They didn't slow, nor did Blue Spur look back. But she huffed a sarcastic chuckle. "Smart boy. Yeah, somewhere above us but below the street and walls, the Dead Pipes are still shuttling that rotten water back and forth."

"My history teacher taught me that the aqueducts were capped millennia ago, to spare the First City's surviving citizens from the poison that was introduced from the Mountain Worship rebels. They went instead to wells and raised piping after that for water, and *magique* Water Singers to monitor it."

"Another bright student. Those pipes were leaded and capped and buried a long time ago. And most of the wells are done too by now. Now we art-pump seawater up from the far port and it gets filtered at the Lilac Reservoir by the Empire's best purification casters. The pipes were blocked up and finished a good two thousand years ago. What of it?"

"Then where is the water going back and forth from?"

No answer. As that trickle noise remained constant, never getting closer or going farther and never revealing its source to the eye or the lantern light, Pon-Chai felt that coldness he'd previously only had at his back change form and turn into a scared mouse, running pawprints down his spine.

*

Even his mental clock gave up and let its sundial shadow go flying as they probed through the dark of the tunnel for hours more. There were a few more turns but otherwise their direction remained the same, away from the city.

They started to slope up sharply, almost steeply, and he found his calf and thigh muscles actually aching from the exertion. Blue Spur said nothing, indicated not even by a greater intake of breath that it was any stress to her. The lantern swung harder as she swung her arm more to keep balance at the greater angle, the light going in crazy arcs.

And the trickle sound of water still with them, as constant as a summer gnat trapped in the sweat behind the ear.

Far sooner than he'd thought, he nearly ran into her back, the lantern doused in a heartbeat.

"Sssss!" She flapped a hand back at him. He was already blinking, restoring his night vision. His ears pricked at the sound of something rustling, the clatter of what sounded like dry sticks being played, bones a-clatter in a sack. Then his eyes cleared and he saw that they seemed to be head-height to the ground...and above them was some scattered assemblage of lights, shadows...triangular slits and cuts...

A fast clicking. And then the entire mass of shadows and slits of light rose at a side angle, propelled by Blue Spur's free hand. He moved around her and up the last few carved-in steps to the surface.

They were in a small copse of stunted dwarf pine. The cover for the end of the tunnel was some sort of false deadfall pile of driftwood, as if various twigs and logs of the trees had been collected then abandoned by some woodsmen. The air redolent of pine needles and sap, the tang of an early dawn chill dewing his lips.

Blue Spur followed him, throwing up the cover and letting it drop behind her with a much quieter puff and clatter than he'd expected for such a mass.

Ah, there's the trick of it. That puff and hiss as it descended and slowed before hitting ground. A layer of light canvas secured up inside the shell of the twigs and lumber...like a sail catching the breeze. Immediately braking the whole thing from landing at full weight. Ingenious. Efficient and ingenious.

Blur Spur grunted, bent down, a few more clickings as she did something that secured the cover from idly blowing up with a strong gale and being discovered. Then she straightened. "Let's get moving while we still have dark on our side."

The logger paths were fairly simple. He could have picked out the strongest of them from those that had been long abandoned even without Blue Spur's guidance. But allowed her her lead and took the opportunity of traveling level ground once more to catch his wind.

They left the copse of trees and passed along the paths through a larger grove before emerging outside of a seven foot wall of packed adobe clay, with sharp spikeheads decorating its top edge. She continued to lead him around to the eastern gate of a sequestered assembly of tidily built log houses.

"What is this place's map-name?"

"It doesn't have one. The Stork has paid good money for that. We call it Breathe Easy." She allowed a snicker to escape. The gate was closed but not locked, so they slipped within.

All the buildings were dark except for one close to the gate as they entered. It had a single hooded lantern in blue-tinged glass panes propped in the open windowframe underneath its awning. Blue Spur led him to this house and knocked on the door in three rapid hummingbird taps.

It was answered immediately by a small-built man who struck Pon-Chai as strangely familiar though he knew they'd never met. He moved aside to give them entry, closing the door quietly and taking down the lantern.

"I'm going back to check if there are any messages left at the outer gate," Blue Spur asserted and walked back out. Before she closed the door, she regarded the men curtly. "This is our way station host. I recommend you get moving as soon as possible again if you hope to catch up with Bent Flute. Even on foot, that woman has a good day's journey ahead of you."

"The woman you brought the other night?" The way station host shook his head. "Oh, no, she left on horseback."

Blue Spur frowned. "What? You don't keep stock here."

"She was met here. Two others. She left with them." Blue Spur shook her head to show the inconsequence this was for her, and closed the door.

"Who met her?" Pon-Chai asked.

A shrug. The man had a decidedly birdish blink to his slow, sleepy regard of his early-morning guest. "A woman, a man. Nothing special."

"By what way did they leave?"

"They only had a horse between them. They put her on it and walked it out of town. They took the Galloping Steed Road, that runs almost all the way to Reipan district."

Reipan. Those years of gazing at atlases opened in his mind, as clean and crisp as cracking open the newest edition in his very hands.

"Would you like something to drink?"

Pon-Chai nodded. "Yes, thank you. Some water to help my throat. The run was very tiring."

The man gave another couple of rapid bird-blinks flashing his eyelids, and stepped outside while Pon-Chai tapped fingers on his knees, sitting and gathering the thoughts that he needed to properly assemble in order to see the whole thing of it.

Reipan was the Annoying Isthmus, according to some older maps. So-named because at the far eastern edge of the Empire jutted an inconvenient finger of mountain ranges. These mountains were stubborn and hard and lifeless to all. No waterfalls to sustain travelers, no thin soil to support even the rudest of mosses or lichen to suck for sustenance. Not a mountain goat's worth of survival there. It was from this same range of mountains, nameless because the Empire never considered them worth officially annexing but instead left them off the official maps, like an illustrated mistake.

But if you traced the faint borderlines, the mountains enjoyed a distinct wraparound of the Reipan district and the Empire's boundary as a whole. The mountain range jutted as a pointed stick into the balloon of the Imperial lands. There were no known passes or tunnels or roads to save any traveler having to go around and through Reipan.

It was from this same range that the Mountain Worship clan of old had legendarily come down, pillaging Reipan before moving slowly on to the capital, carrying the strange mineral powder they'd mined and claimed the Gods Beneath had bequeathed them, charged with the sole person of eliminating all those who sacrilegiously Lived Above in the Air and Blasphemy. The powder they'd poured into the First City's aqueducts, killing untold thousands before it was discovered.

The way station host returned, carrying in one hand a small bucket of well water, and a clay cup in the other already filled. Pon-Chai gave him a grateful nod and took the cup. "You said they were headed to Reipan, I heard that correctly?"

The man tilted his head in thought as he stood by the doorway, in a slack-shouldered posture that almost made it look like this was where he was at-rest when not called for any task; standing beside the door, as still and unbothered as any rack for a coat or hat. "Yes. I'm quite certain that was where they were going. But it goes through some pretty nasty grounds before it reaches there. That Road only gets used to the next town before people usually veer off for other parts. If you stay on the Galloping Steed past that, you have to ride its back through ravine lands and old highwayman haunts. Bad country. Only the mad or the crooked have reason to go that way. Better to add two days' journey to your trip and get to Reipan by way of the Ice Floe River going northerly." Another set of blinks of his somewhat dog-sad large eyes.

"Thank you." A silver flash and was pressed into the man's palm before he knew Pon-Chai had even grasped it to shake and release, jogging past him.

It could only be Reipan that the party was headed for. It was simple and expedient. Because of that mountain range poking itself into the side of the Empire, it represented the single shortest distance anyone could travel from the capital and get to a border. Any other way would have risked being seen and reported by someone loyal to the palace. Reipan was only two days' away by most direct line; any other direction or goal would add days, possibly weeks to their travels, and all still be firmly within the Emperor's infuriated reach. One could reach the furthest intrusion of the mountains into the boundary the fastest...with the added benefit that few would want to go hunting about in such inhospitable grounds as the foothills of the mountain range. Even that was a country of flinty, close-mouthed people fabled for eating their weakest in the thickest of winters as food got scarce, and their oxen were prized more for their lingering strength into the springs than their eldest and sickest for what gristle was left on their cold bones.

He could see the map so clearly, and there was a certainty there he could not have entirely explained. Certainly thieves and brigands had done stupid things, defied logic, failed to go the efficient or competent way in their plans...

...no. The Thinker, the Ladder, the Steady. This was a clear plot, with as few moving parts and mistakes as were possible for something of its scale.

These people had come for her...meaning more that they had been sent. And that suggested yet the final party. Waiting at the window, testing the winds before risking a single toe out on the top rung.

Someone was running this plan, and they could read a map as easily as he.

All right. All right. He saw Blue Spur sitting on a stool by the village gate, the gate itself wide open and moonlight sparkling off ice plants growing to the sides of the road. He stopped and caught his breath.

"All accounted for then? Nothing else?" She had been checking something in her plaited ponytail but as he'd approached had swept it back without explanation. She straightened, tugging down her tunic where it had bunched at her chest. "You paid for here, but I know the Stork liked you so that means I have to at least ask."

"You think he liked me?"

She shook her head. "You're alive, aren't you?"

"Fair. Thank you for your help."

She seemed to have something expected between them. A question like a bee trapped behind a window, not buzzing loud enough to be heard and set free.

"Was there something else?"

She frowned. Seemed to bite her tongue on the question. Then thought again.

"Do you come to the capital often?"

"This was my first visit since I was twelve."

"Why then?"

"My father brought me. He was given an award and wished me to see more of the world."

"Your father?"

"No one of consequence to us here."

"All right then." Her twang seemed to thicken as she lowered her voice. "You weren't the worst person to take out."

"Thank you."

"You didn't need carrying half the way."

"Did Little Wife?"

She nodded. She glanced at the open road beyond the village gate. "Where from here?"

"Better you don't know. Less chance of indiscretions."

"You talk like the Stork."

"He and I had some professional tasks in common."

"Mmm-hmm."

"You were a fine guide."

"Thanks."

He gave her a polite bow, and then was moving past her, already trying to calculate the distance to the curve of road some length away that he would need to avoid in order to go into the roughs of Galloping Steed, and hopefully the conclusion of all this in time.

"Hey."

He stopped and turned back to her.

"Yes?"

"What's wrong with the tunnel trapdoor? If we were raided, you said?"

"It's too obvious. The corridor is narrow, boxed in by the walls. No windows, no outlet to the sky, no ladder. It's an alley where you have no access to a back street or a rooftop, and your employer's eatery puts no trash or anything back there. Just smooth gravel dead-ending into a wall. Any three-quarters-brained junior investigator with the Screaming House would see that and easily suspect there was some unseen purpose to it. Better to at least have a few cans of trash, some old crates off to the side. Or even something on top of the panel that can be easily removed and returned by an attendant as you leave. Make it look more like an accident of the architects who built around the space, than to leave it so clean and yet so clearly built there for a purpose."

"But we won't get raided. The Stork is too powerful. Too many people in the right places are invested in him being kept safe." In the dim, with her voice hushed, this sounded more a litany than an assurance. "And his family here..." but then she snapped her mouth shut on that last, immediately looking rueful of the mistake.

Then the way station guide's eyes, his blinks, his careful regard and even elements of his posture and speech. "Ah...our host is the Stork's brother, isn't he?"

She glowered at him, then visibly relented and only permitted a single terse tip of her chin to confirm.

That's one way to best guarantee a safe depot, I suppose. "But that's why I know the Stork's holdings will never be subject to any raid."

Pon-Chai shrugged. "Then my suggestions are worthless to you. No worry." A cough to clear his throat of the last of that dank tunnel air permeating his lungs. The well water had helped revive him a great deal. "Still, though...the Dead Pipes still run, despite being buried and stilled so long ago."

"What does that have to do with it?" Some of her old manner crept back in. A stray waft of moonlight sprayed off her silver needles.

"Perhaps nothing. But it makes me respect that that which is buried...has a way of eventually being heard by the wrong ears. Despite all precautions and presumptions otherwise."

He left her with that, as he began to jog towards the Galloping Steed Road. And soon enough she was gone on her own way back to the capital. And her long—hopefully uneventful—journey under its oldest horrors.

They wouldn't feel too much need to cover their trail, from here to Reipan. Not if they figured she got to them covertly already. And with at least a day or more's lead on everyone, who could suspect?

No...consider it differently. As he jogged, keeping himself hopping from the ball of one feet to the other and back again, he let the rhythm enforce some patter and order to his thinking.

Use all the facts, not just the sweetest peaches that fell off the branch.

All right then. By the time she'd gotten out of the capital, it was already three days from the theft. The city was locked down but no news leaked of the loss. Whoever came for her must have truly thought themselves safe from anyone following, once they confirmed she had gotten this far.

So they would have felt safe, but not so safe they would take the longer route to Reipan and add the time or risk exposure in the villages along that route. And the destination was chosen for its closeness to start with. Everything suggested they would take the more forlorn road.

It was going to be dawn before he expected to make any distance and gain back something from his prey.

*

They have a horse. But they were walking the woman on its back. So they will be only as fast as the slowest of them leading the animal.

At a conservative jog to conserve his energy and avoid as much risk of accident as possible, Pon-Chai reached the Ice Floe detour curve by nightfall of the first day.

Here he had to stop for a better rest than sitting a few minutes at a time every few miles. He took the time to walk around in a widening spiral from where the road forked and diverted into the well-kept path onto the detour, and the more weed-wracked one that continued over the next hills on the more direct but dangerous route to Reipan.

Useless to look for horse track in the dirt or gravel. No telling how fresh a track is even if you see one.

Then his eye spotted something green amongst the brown and gray of the soil and gravel. An apple, nearly finished. The top and bottom of the core still showed golden-green skin. The bites were wide like shovel bites.

The horse at least has eaten something. He hunched down and examined the core, picking it up and sniffing it. Still fragrant. He ran a finger along the exposed meat of it. Soft. Rotting, but not wholly rotten yet. The skin and flesh were pocked with brown fingerprint marks of decay...but when he pressed a fingernail into the meat and dug a little, the nail came back wet. Still with juice.

Less than a day's distance, then. The weather had been neither too dry nor too wet, a remarkably balance climate here...so the apple couldn't have been tossed away all that long before he came.

He tossed the apple away and found a hummock of high-grass. The shallow rise, combined with its wheat-colored golden grasses, afforded him some cover from the road if he stretched out on the ground behind it and didn't raise his head too high. He took the encouragement of the apple core to catch an hour's sleep.

Before he was able to allow his thoughts to go completely quiet and go back into the midnight-draped room of his mind where no sound or light struck until he would choose to wake again, he heard a field dog's stray cry to the rising crescent moon. It caused him to hesitate in his rest, considering the risks.

They have easier prey out there than to come up on me asleep. He let his eyes become stone and his ears became empty conch shells, transmitting nothing to the mind behind them to disturb it.

*

The moon had marked an hour's arc and Pon-Chai awoke. He confirmed no one was around, stretched a few moments, then began to jog along the rougher road to the forests before the Annoying Isthmus' mountain range.

He had to move slower and more carefully owing to the weeds and occasional deadfalls in the disused road. The moonlight was still strong enough that he could pick out the white gravel the road had been originally strewn with, almost like snowdrifts amongst the shadows. The road followed the uneven rolling hills, causing him to tire faster with the exertions of handling the poor grades up and down.

The forests seemed to not so much gradually come closer as try and spring upon him, like bandits hiding. He took the summit of a nastily high hill and as he crested it, there below the rise was the beginning of the forests. The trees marched themselves at the foot of the hill with no warning or subtlety. He paused to consider the road going down into the trees.

His eyes picked out the faintest indigo smear of open space where the road sloped down and cut through the trees. Weeds and grasses may have grown, but thankfully there were no fresh saplings breaking up the road to make it even harder to pick out in the dim. He followed this down, the forest enveloping him in a pine-and-burnt-oak-smelling blanket of near-silence.

It was halfway through the night, as told by spotting slivers of the moon through the canopy of boughs, when he came upon the side road, and the cabin it led to a score of yards off the main venue. The telltale flicker—only a moment, here and then gone in a blink and he'd almost missed it entirely trying to keep the road under him—of firelight reflecting off the inside of a cloudy glass-paned window amidst the branches to his left.

Immediately he jumped off the road and found a space between the densely-bunched trees to hide himself where he could still see the road as well as the cabin.

He picked his way along the clear spaces to the cabin.

A huge shadow-demon loomed up, about to swallow the world and fall over him, tackling him—

He jerked back as the massive shadow nickered, gave a derisive snort from its long head. His eyes made out the twitch of ears, the mane.

The horse. A heavy-hoofed breed, just right for the foothills territory.

How many hands tall? It turned its head and a jewel eye regarded him. A sniff. A huff of breath as it clopped one hoof against the ground.

There was a narrow corridor of cleared ground around the cabin. The horse was tied and almost filled this space on the side of the cabin.

He ventured a pat to the side of its neck, gave a very calming whistle-sigh to it that it seemed to accept. It didn't respond as he moved around it and towards the front of the cabin. Merely lowered its head and resumed chewing on what grasses it found there.

He slipped to the window, peering in. The glass was of poor quality but it was clear enough to see that there was some light shuddering up against another window in the side wall. That allowed the sight of someone inside by the stove. The rest was too much shadows to see anything.

He held still and put the fingertips of a hand spider-soft against a lower corner of glass. Stilled himself.

Everything was through his fingertips. He closed his eyes. He let merely the sensations through his fingertips try and paint the room on a canvas of his mind.

There was a sharp snap of wood popping in a fire. *But the light is too low...a stove? Yes. A stove.*

He was trying to hear for anything giving away the presences that could be in the cabin. But there was no rustling, no clicks and clacks of a camp plate being eaten off of. No low hiss-scrape of someone sharpening a knife or idly stropping a dagger. No snoring, no flatulence.

He removed his fingertips from the glass, noting the rosette of small white moons of oil he'd left there.

He took the risk to slide along the wall to the front door. Lowered himself in line with the bottom of the door and looked in. A very low vermilion sliver of the stove light. He took a slow, deep breath and smelled must, woodsmoke, a little apple as of the golden-green variety he'd found a core for earlier.

But other than the cloudy figure he'd seen by the light source, there was maddeningly no indications he could trust as to whether or not there was anyone else inside.

"You idiot!"

The yell was so loud in the stillness of the woods that Pon-Chai's heart doubled its beat a minute before his ears and brain corroborated that the cry had come from somewhere behind him and off deeper into the woods behind the cabin. The trees were so close, echoes carried more weight for longer distances here.

"Shut up!"

The first had been a woman's voice. The reply, snarled but still loud in the gloaming depths, was a man's.

There are my two escorts. But why are they out—

A crackling of disturbed underbrush. The pat-pat pattern in the thumps of something with four legs. He could tell from the most minute timing of the thump-thumps and the crackles that it was probably some sort of stag or deer.

Poaching. Of course. While their cargo stays in the cabin, they're off hunting deer in the night. They couldn't have brought many rations with them for this journey.

If that was so, this was his only opportunity while they were otherwise distracted.

Inside the cabin, the woman sat in a miserable pile of filthy clothes. For a beat, he was almost paused to think this was the beggar-mother of the alley put before him again. But no...she was sleepless and haggard, but much paler and cleaner than that woman had been (by a narrow margin). She sat hunched not for a pregnant belly but simply for lack of energy left in her spine to hold her straighter. The feeble firelight of the cabin's meager tin stove flickered against her as if it wasn't sure of touching her anymore than any human would be.

He closed the door quietly behind him and stood before her.

Do it swift, before she can raise any alarms or put up any fight. Yes. But the hunched and defeated thing here seemed utterly incapable of either action, or any other.

He took two steps closer, trying to discern more detail from the stovelight.

A log in the stove crackled, spat up an ember from its stovetop lid. The woman looked up at last, noticing his presence.

"Are you Little Wife Bent Flute?"

She didn't respond. Only stared.

"Are you the midwife-assistant who fled the palace five days ago?"

Nothing.

He dared another step closer.

"Do you carry something with you? Something that should not be carried further?"

Her eyes closed.

"Where is it?"

She inclined her head. Her hair fell over her face, turning it into a mask of black.

"Where is it?"

A faint, breathy keening emerged from under the hair. It gasped away in seconds. The sound of something in pain, but so tired as to nearly be at the point where the body was too spent to even feel that brightness in its nerves.

She shook her head.

"I am sorry, but I must know where it is."

None of this felt right. Three Brooms was no longer speaking from the rear-thoughts of memory and caution, but his gnarled brown hand was striking the back of Pon-Chai's head with the alarm of it.

This is a fool's contract. Leave it.

But I am here. After so much effort.

Effort's nothing. Live to tell the tale of your failure, don't die successful. Leave it.

"Please. I don't wish to hurt you—"

Liar. You will.

"—but I must know where it is, and have it from you."

Again, the silent shake of the head.

Untaught. But Untaught did not mean ashamed. It did not automatically mean undisciplined, or truly unlearned. To have served as a midwife to a royal physician this woman must have been capable of a great many wise things. She must have...been capable of giving directions as well as taking them...

...Bent Flute.

He swiftly moved forward, kneeling to a knee and thrusting his hand into the darkness, feeling the chin there, tucked against the collarbone. He pulled, softly but undeniably, and brought her face up to meet his. In the stove's pathetic illumination, the dirt around her eyes made golgothas of her sockets. Her mouth was caked at the corners...

She wouldn't eat anything in the safehouses.

She had to wait two days to leave. She's been on the path for three since then.

I christened her Little Wife Bent Flute. On account of that lack of a flapping mouth of hers.

Gods and fates and all the cursed things that ever defied them...what fresh atrocity was this?

It was blood at the edges of her mouth. Very softly, as gently as all his art could allow him, Pon-Chai curled his hand around her chin, and used his fingers and thumb to press at the gaunt hollows of her cheeks.

A tear squeezed from the corner of an eye, and there was a gasp of tired air from the bellows of her lungs. But otherwise she did nothing to protest or fight him as her lips pursed and then parted with a faint, nauseating tearing noise...like wet tissue...

Clotted blood flaked from her lips, pattered onto his wrist.

The chasm of her mouth exhaled a breath that was oily, coppery and rotted. But her teeth that he saw were pearly and still healthy...and then he realized he could see the mid-teeth towards the back of the lower jaw...

...because there was no tongue there to block his sight.

Instead, where her tongue should have rested like a pale catfish in its burrow, there was a glint of steel.

Stainless. They cut out her tongue and affixed a stainless steel cylinder to the bottom of her mouth...he did not want to examine too deeply to work out how the cylinder had been secured there...possibly stitched, but he saw no telltale criss-crossing of any wire or silk over the cylinder as he turned her head towards the stove for better light.

This was done with some knowledge. And she was like this when Blue Spur took charge of her. Did the Stork have one of his other 'experts' at task first? To prepare her for the journey as a living satchel? Or some other party in the court that was part of the plot? This all gets uglier the longer the path winds its way.

Suddenly her exhaustion and utter lack of resistance clicked into place as neatly as the cog workings of a mechanical clock.

Five days. This blood is dried.

She wasn't speaking or eating when Blue Spur hid her...five days with no food...perhaps only the thinnest trickle of water directly down her upturned throat to keep her going. But no way to eat while that precious cargo was sealed inside her mouth.

She has been slowly starving to death while carrying this burden further away from the palace.

"I am very sorry for this." He meant every word. "You were a part of a horrible plot...but no Steady deserves this, no woman or man on earth deserves to be abused in this manner for theft. Not in the toolship of another's plan. I am sorry."

It had to come out. He had to see it. He was certain it would be there, and be what the Third Minister and his superiors feared it was. But he had to be sure. It was the crucial third of his contract.

Kill the thief. Get the name. Bring it back.

If he took this all the way back and it proved to be a blank strip of paper, or nothing at all inside that cylinder, this would all have been for a waste.

Including what this poor woman has already suffered.

He tried to peer harder to see the method of how the cylinder was affixed, but could only see that it did not roll or move with her head, but stayed perfectly still at the bottom of her mouth.

"I am sorry," he said again. He meant it even more this time.

She closed her eyes.

Better now than after more pain. More indignity.

He lunged forward, his free hand coming up, swinging around to cup the back of her head, bringing her face to his chest almost like a father welcoming home a long-lost daughter. As he did so, his hand holding her jaw snapped in the opposite direction, against the leverage of the hand on the back of her head that firmly jerked counterclockwise to further propel the whole thing too far, too fast, the neck snapping with a crumpled sound of something stepping on a glass wrapped in soft cotton.

It was fast, it was muffled in the folds of his sleeves and tunic breast. She didn't make a sound. The weakest galvanic shiver ran through her body, and then there was nothing from her any longer. Before his hand released the back of her neck, moving down to gently lower her to the floor. The whole motion was almost a sad dance capitulating into this final dip and soft drop. The suitor had left his love asleep on the ground.

But it was no bower of flowers or sleepy bedroom setting, as his father might have written, that he was to leave her in. Merely a musty cabin in the middle of hinterlands. Possibly to even be undiscovered until the next lonesome traveler needed shelter.

Damn it.

Damn it? Three Brooms smiled nastily from the swimming dark of his rear-thoughts. *No. Damn* me, *you mean.*

Yes, sir. Damn me.

That was struck. The first part of the contract. Now to get the rest of the sorry business over with.

He prized open the mouth, and with barely a pause or further regret had jerked the cylinder free of the mouth with a moist noise, a slurp like the vacuum of pulling a boot from mud. Some sort of pine glue? Something that would not dissolve and tasted disgusting so as to not encourage over-salivating and possibly seeping into the cylinder to ruin its value?

Don't analyze. Now the voice was bizarrely that of Mother Blue Spur rather than his old master. *If you're not going to listen and leave this now, get it done swiftly at least. Fool.*

Agreed. The cylinder bounced once in his testing hand, feeling its tiny weight.

It was not a lockable cylinder; he inspected it for glyphs, any ricecutter ideograms that might be minutely carved on it to ward off or punish anyone improperly opening it.

It unscrewed along a fine, hair-thin seam at the center. He twisted and the cylinder popped into open halves. With a rough twist of yellowed and grimed paper inside.

He took a breath. Another.

Do I do this? Professional integrity says of course. But to know this? There is no killer to hire for the memories of one's own mind. And I am not inclined to cut my own tongue out after.

You are only as vulnerable as you allow others to see you to be. That you give them the capabilities to do you hurt. Three Brooms scratched his patchy beard, Pon-Chair's ears nearly hearing for real that rasp as he smiled from a dead man's corner of the mind. *Why like any obvious child would you assume that only applies to temptations and pains from* without?

Pon-Chai sighed. *Things were so much simpler when all my task was was to kill. Moral dilemmas are far simpler to dismiss when they are done-or-not-done. Not this limbo of constant decision.*

He began to unroll the twist of paper.

The door behind him slammed open. He spun, hands moving and arms going out, feet wide in a balanced stance.

The woman was in the front. The man behind her was a head taller than her and had something dead slung over his shoulders, which he shrugged to the ground the moment they had seen him.

"Who the hell...?" The woman stepped into the threshold. Her eyes took in the stove, the dead woman on the floor, back to Pon-Chai. The thiefkiller said nothing. "*What have you done?*"

"What can't be undone," Pon-Chai answered quietly. "So we may fight or we may talk."

"You're a dead man. Do you have any idea who you've crossed?"

"You are welcome to enlighten me."

She sneered at him. "The wrong people, that's all you need to know."

The woman had a bearing not unlike Mother Blue Spur. Yet she was years younger, more slender-built. But she had the same manner of dressing for practical, brute competence. Her clothes were a stained and patched wool, stained some dark tones that her partner's clothing matched. Her hair was cropped short almost to the skull. There was a deep and ugly scar that cut across her jawline, as if someone had inexpertly tried to cut her throat. She held a shortsword in her hand, pointed towards him, and he saw the top of a bow slung at her back. He couldn't see what her partner may have been carrying.

"Defying the Emperor's court would, I think, make you no doubt in the wrong."

"The capital is two days' journey back from us now. Unless you are hiding your army in the trees, you aren't leaving here."

"Why did you have to brutalize the woman? She was clearly no threat to you."

"She did her job. She copied down the name and brought it to us." The woman shook her head, a similar rueful gesture he would have seen from Blue Spur. "Cow thought we'd pay her and be done. She didn't expect to be the pigeon for the whole trip."

"She was Untaught. All physician assistants are. How—"

"You're a schoolboy, aren't you?" The sneer widened, turning the face into an ugly mask. The man spat on the ground behind her. "All you highborn fools are the same. We are Untaught, not stupid."

"I do not assume Untaught is stupid."

"Spare me. You assume Untaught is still foolish. A woman who could not read or write, but you give no credit to the idea that she could have memorized what she saw and re-draw it, like any sketch, to take out with her?"

"Ah." Pon-Chai nodded. "It is so plain that I am the one that is foolish indeed." The thiefkiller shrugged. "It is a shame, then, if you did not take the time in your flight to copy the name."

"What do you mean?"

He showed his open hands, and waved his right towards the grill front of the small stove. "I mean that I have already destroyed the name that the women held in her mouth before you returned."

The woman's eyes bulged as she looked at the stove.

The man behind her never got to say a word.

When she glanced away from him, Pon-Chai swung his left hand forward. His wrist snapped with the movement to add thrust but also lend a slight curve to the release, giving it an upward angle even as the hand and arm had dipped to give it the most strength in its swing.

Something steely-blue, a flash of ocean water in the gloom of the cabin, parted the air between himself and the man standing in the doorway.

The throwing dart was shaped something like a teardrop, a tapered tip of a couple inches that belled out into a rounded mid-body weight for balance, then terminated in a more snub-nosed tapered tip, needle-fine. A single one of these darts was heavier than it looked. It was shorter than the throwing darts in a tavern, and all smooth metal with no threaded parts nor vanes or feathers to help guide it.

You have to throw it by sheer force at what you intend to hit. The craftsman, a genius known as Valorous Metal Beekeeper, *had cautioned him about their finicky nature. They will fly smooth and true, but they will not fly on their own.*

Does the tip have a reservoir or a scrolling to hold poison?

These are not tools for lazy hobbyists and amateurs, boy. If you throw one of these hard enough to strike and strike true and know what you're doing, poison is a weak second to the cobra-strike death these will render unto another.

Pon-Chai always carried some concealed in his sleeves. The smooth small shapes were easy enough to allow to carefully slide along pre-sewn channels in his clothing so he could lift his arms for a body search, or slide his arms down and let one fall down into the cuff to hide. A slide slither-shake of that same arm, and the weak strand of stitching would part to allow the tiny projectile to fall soundlessly into his waiting palm. By the genius of Metal Beekeeper's craftsmanship, that snubbed nose somehow had a diamond-fine tip yet the bulbous middle-body created enough wave ahead of its form that the tip never snagged in any of his clothes no matter how often he'd needed to keep them hidden on his person in one corner of a tunic or another.

Valorous Metal Beekeeper had insisted that with proper practice, nothing living would survive a strike from one of his 'little bees.'

And Pon-Chai had practiced tirelessly with them until there was no thought or hesitation in aiming. This was only the fourth time he'd had need to use one of his hidden friends. It was the fourth time that Beekeeper had still proven absolutely true.

The dart struck the man high in his throat, almost where the Adam's apple met the beginning up-curve sweep of the bottom of the jaw. With the upward angle and thrust imparted on it, the tiny thing made of the preternaturally heavy and dense alloy pierced his throat and left a hole faster than the eye could have registered that something had struck there (Beekeeper insisted it was a steel mixture that had a personal recipe of a 'sky-rock' mineral added that made the metal so heavy for such tiny scale).

The tip was still diamond-fine. It parted flesh and tendon, windpipe and arteries. It could not pierce and continue on from the back of the man's head, but when it met bone and nerve fiber it stopped, lodged there and instantly stilling the man's body.

Pon-Chai did not watch to gloat over his marksmanship. As his hand had released the dart, he let his weight succumb to gravity behind him. Legs loosening and his back relaxing, he went into a kind of backwards somersault, his backside taking the brunt of hitting the ground to smooth the lower part of his spine curving and rolling back.

He was rolling to the back wall of the cabin, out of the meager stove light and into the shadow.

Some shadows deeper than others that a man may get lost in them. Here was hoping the Stork's wisdom was not simply talk.

But he had not counted on the dead woman's leg being stuck out at the right distance to catch his right buttock. It threw him off balance. Instead of rolling back and into a crouch in the shadowed back of the cabin as intended he instead was in a lopsided roll that brought him into an ungainly crash against that wall. Something in the dark struck his head. A moldering piece of firewood for the stove? It didn't matter, it was hard enough to make him hiss air between his teeth and know that a respectable knot would show up on the back of his head.

The woman at the door was not slow of instinct or indecisive. She didn't even look to her companion collapsing to the ground, falling outside the doorway. She lurched forward at him, shortsword coming up to give her room for a deadly swing.

Her clothing was not only for travel. He saw as her arm moved that there was a flattened shift to the upper and lower arms...some sort of boiled leather plate affixed in segments within the clothes. Covert armor. Basic, but effective and hidden. His head throbbed.

She swung, with the skill to know to make a diagonal slash down towards him, rather than a roundhouse flat swing he could duck. He had to snap in reverse, his back squeezed to the wall, throwing himself down and to the right to narrowly her blow in the confines of the cabin.

His foot automatically kicked out, but that bruised foot had not fully recovered, and the last day and night's running had done it no good. A blaze of pain spiked up from the arch of his foot as it made contact with her stomach and more of that hard, unseen plating. The woman whoofed and doubled. He tried to move forward, to take her there, but she recovered faster and made a clumsy backhand sweep of the shortsword, clubbing against his shoulder and nearly finding his head. The blow's contact threw her off-balance and he took advantage of the moment's stagger against the other far cabin wall to reach the doorway.

A glance down told him the dead man was useless. If he'd been carrying a blade of his own, it was still strapped and somewhere under his body. There wasn't time to do any search. Pon-Chai took a leaping step over the corpse and was moving for the path back to the road.

Only a breath sounded behind him before lightning slammed through his skull and sent him down. As with his foot, the blow he'd taken in the dark to the back of the head was only made worse by whatever this new assault was.

He went down to all fours, hissing air as his teeth clenched, face pale with all his energy to move seemingly whirlpooled away down the vortex of this swallowing, crackling, spark-spraying agony playing between his ears.

"Not the swift smart talker now."

He heard the rustle-thump of her plate-sewn clothes approach. Then there was a final blast, lightning that had steel dart tines at the ends of its bolts into his head, and he went completely dark.

The first thing to awaken are ears.

Pon-Chai heard the ground-fog of reedy insect noises. His nostrils took in a sour-sweet smell of watery earth. Mossy. A sigh told him of trees overhead, but it was the faintest plip that revealed water. Still water. But it wasn't raining—

He was laying on a side. His arms were pinioned behind him. He risked a motion of shrugging to feel the bite of coarse rope looped and knotted around his forearms. The tightest was at his wrists and the rope ended just below his elbows.

She tied me in a funnel formation. Amateur, but annoying.

He ventured to open his eyes.

The sky overhead was still visible as fits and starts of a dark violet night with barely any moonlight. There was one opening, something like a starfish where the longest boughs didn't meet. Overhead, he could make out four stars...five...a rough trapezoid in the heavens...

The Hunter's Skirt. High. It's late. I've been out at least an hour.

He was lying in a space of clear dirt. Slightly sandy. A rock or pebble was wedging against his stomach. There was a pond. Small, really more of a spring except it was still. Possibly a flood swamp? No, there were no trees or anything in the water. This had been here a while. The small clearing he lay in further attested to that.

As he surveyed his surroundings, a doe came and drank at the far edge of the pond from him. He watched her silently.

Was it your buck who they killed, perhaps? Your fawn? Even if so, you won't necessarily feel the heartache, the logical fears that should extrapolate from that for yourself, will you? Simpler life.

Her head jerked up. The doe's huge eyes darted back and forth, and with a massive leap she was gone into the shadows.

The rustling and breaking of brush. Grunts, the rasp of fabric across bark and dirt. From out of view emerged the woman, hunched and trudging backwards. Dragging.

She dragged the dead woman onto the sandy soil and dropped her next to him with a gasp and suck of air.

"You're awake." She chuckled. "That'll be a bit harder for you then."

"Your plans would be softer in the event of my being asleep?"

"I've heard drowning tends to be peaceful when one is already asleep."

The funnel, then. He rolled so that he was further on his back. "You'll drown me? Rather than take me back to your superiors to account for your failure?"

She kicked him in the stomach. It was a hard kick and he'd already rolled too far back, so instead of the stomach she mostly caught his side. A bruising blow that left him gasping for several moments. She laughed and took the time of his recovery to hunt around for stones to start shoving in the dead woman's ragged pockets.

"You...find failure...funny?"

"I haven't failed, you lying bastard." She left the dead woman's sinking preparations and lunged over to him. She leaned down and waved a familiar twist of paper in his face. "Nice trick. And you have quite a few other fun little things in your pockets too, don't you?" She plucked out one of the blue-steeled darts and waggled it in front of him. "Your cute tools are all stripped. Now lay quiet and perhaps I'll do you the favor of hitting you upside the head again with my feupol and let you drown in peace."

A feupol. Of course. A device of some ingenuity along the lines of the Beekeeper's darts, if a bit cruder in conception. Take a small velvet or cotton bag of two or three inches to a side and sew inside it securely a measure of iron ball bearings. This small but heavy item could then be itself sewn into the lining of a sleeve cuff. In a rushed moment of pursuit, the practiced wearer could use it as a last minute bola device. Use the fist to clutch up the slack of the cuff and swing the arm, snapping hard in a motion similar to a throwing knife toss or one of the Beekeeper's little bees. The small bean bag of iron would easily snap the thin stitching, flying forward. With selection of the right spot—the back of the knee or head—the quarry could be brought down handily.

Pon-Chai had once practiced for a week with a feupol himself, during a long year's study of various weaponry both overt and subtle. A feupol had savage merits. And had this woman gotten her metal from the Beekeeper, his strange sky-rock blued alloy, the one she'd used to bring him down could as easily have gone through his skull than knock him out.

But the iron was noisy if you moved too much, like hearing marbles rolling inside one's sleeve. And there was no way to shift the packet once stitched into place, such as during body searches in government offices or local governors' mansions. He'd rejected it as useless to his work.

Clearly this woman as a hired hand needed no such subtleties.

She'd taken his knives, his lockpicks, his other darts. She could not have found his poisons, as the packets were sewn from the same fabric as the lining inside the lapel of his tunic and so skillfully interwoven there that no one could find them if they didn't know they were there. But poisons weren't going to do any good. He doubted she would untie him if he asked for a last request and wished to be permitted to brew tea for her. And she had recovered the name. That was now a refreshed priority.

It would have to be a certain amount of wit, then.

"You are Untaught. The name is meaningless to you. It doesn't occur to you that your employer will merely dispose of you...perhaps in some pond elsewhere like this one?"

"Shut up." She was apparently out of rope and attempting to fashion some sort of knotting wrap around the dead woman's ankles to hold onto a good-sized rock she'd discovered.

"The name could be anything, have you considered that?"

She paused in her frustrated winding of grasses. "What are you talking about?"

"You are right that many learned people underestimate an Untaught. The midwife no doubt did it as you said, exactly. To draw out the ideograms and letters as basic shapes and lines. Even an Untaught could learn the deft hand of basic calligraphy, without comprehending a single letter or word."

"So?"

"So there is still the matter of actually knowing, absolutely knowing, that what she copied is indeed a name and not...some physician's notation of a bad bowel movement that day. Or a script for an apothecary mixture to be sent for and brought back to help the pregnant Empress with her foul stomach winds."

"She got the name," the woman snapped. But her eyes suggested he was talking to the right person for doubt. There was supposedly no honor amongst thieves, but Three Brooms' first lesson to him had been that honor begins within one's own mind. She trusted nothing, including her own place in the world. It must have taken a lot for a woman to be of any merit for employment in a cutthroat business. But that seemed to breed greater fear, not confidence.

"You seem quite certain, given the haphazard nature of how all this has gone so far."

"There's nothing hazardous about it. That was the plan from the beginning."

"But the writing still could have been anything in that moment. She had no way to confirm it truly was the name."

The woman practically threw the dead woman's feet to the ground in her disgust. "She told us. The Second Physician Frightened Wolf was her employer. He needed the name to make sure that some mixture of salve he was making with *magique* wouldn't interrupt one of the other chirurgeon's spells for good-fortune in birth. He told her to burn it, and she threw it into the fire under armed guard. But she memorized it well enough to get it written down when she left the palace that night. It's the Heir Emperor's name and you trying to convince me otherwise is a waste of chatter and your voice is giving me a headache."

He continued unperturbed. "No doubt Second Physician Frightened Wolf was one of the first servants killed when the court discovered the loss. So fortunate, then, that you can be so assured. Then again, if you are wrong and all this is hinged on an illiterate midwife trusting a piece of paper long burned in a fire, perhaps your employer will have a permanent solution for all your headaches when you arrive at his doorstep."

"Shut up," she ordered again, and went back to working on the makeshift ropes around the corpse's ankles.

"Would you consider a trade?"

"You're not leaving alive, so shut it."

He fell quiet there. She successfully secured the rock to the cadaver's ankles. Now she began to walk the circle of the clearing, trying to find something else similarly weighty to attach to the body elsewhere. He rolled all the way to his back to follow her with his eyes. The pebble dug into his side a bit less. That much was a relief.

The Hunter's Skirt was moving. Time was still short.

"You have another body to dispose of, I believe?"

"My partner goes on the horse," the woman muttered back, still looking in the brush for something. She found a piece of petrified log, shook it in her grip a little to test the weight, nodded to herself. She came back to the corpse, at it's head this time, her back to the water. "His people will want his body for proper burial."

"Quite a sentiment from a hired mercenary for another."

"They paid me for it, if it happened. Both our families did. Nobody's using our guts for spell-powders or to make a zeit-chu of our bones."

Old country superstitions. The enslaved flesh of the dead, twisted into ghost dogs to join a wizard's hunting pack for children or nubile women. Guts fried and burnt until the last ashes could be collected and sold to novice spellcasters to snort, and in the supposed ensuing euphoria gain greater insight into how to cast larger m'agique. More and more it was clear he was not dealing with any urbanite sophisticate of killers.

He rolled back to his side to face her. "So the woman goes into the pond, the man goes onto the horse, and you go to your employer with nothing."

"Shut up!" She marched over and gave him another kick. This one not as hard. She was rushed.

Good. Be in a hurry.

He took some breaths, making them louder than necessary as she returned to trying to repeat the trick with the reeds knotted around the piece of wood to the dead woman's neck.

He let her fumble at the attempt for long minutes. A lone cricket tried to set up a solo performance but seemed to tire of the effort quickly and give it up as lost.

"I am not proposing a trade for my life. For my death."

The woman stopped and glared at him. "What?"

"If you will agree to...dispatch me in a faster manner, a cleaner way...I will look upon the name and confirm if it is, indeed, the prize you believe you have."

"That's an idiot's bargain."

"How so?" Pon-Chai's voice was light, as conversational as negotiating a suitable time to meet for a theater show. "You don't need to untie me or change anything to hold the paper in front of me. And I have no desire to suffer the agony of drowning."

"You could simply lie to me and tell me it isn't."

"You're forgetting one thing."

"Oh?" Another sneer turned into a chuckle.

"The *m'agique* of a virtuous name."

She fully paused in her ministrations to the corpse and stared at him. "What?"

There it is. The proper voice. The voice that is low and everything it utters ends as a question. Go on.

"The *m'agique* of the Heir Emperor's virtuous name." Still, he spoke as if they were debating a popular lyre-player's performance. "It is a binding power inherent in the very syllables. It is impossible to look upon without a sense of commitment to it as the true name of its bearer. An Untaught cannot read it and so the charm does not work. But any person who is learned and can read it, who lays eyes upon it, cannot deny what it is, even if we do not invoke the name for anything else." Now he dropped all casualness out of his speech and locked unblinking eyes with her. "If you show me the name, there is no way under Heaven's Spires or above a Devil's Coals that I can lie and say it is anything but what it truly is."

"And yet for all this..." the woman's voice was still the right low voice. Considering. "...you would actually trade me simply killing you quickly?"

Pon-Chai nodded. "I have no illusions when I face a professional killer. I will die. And frankly, if I see the Heir Emperor's name...I know I will be tempted to try and use it in some way, the same as your employer or whomever they will sell the name to. And I am not a thinker. I am not a schemer of any merit. You caught me out, that should alone be proof of that. I'm a thief, nothing more. A good one, perhaps, but now that career ends. If you show it to me, and it truly is the name, it's just as well that I bargain for some form of finish and not be sent off to my own temptations. I will be caught...and I hear the Screaming House has ways of letting a dying man go on for years in one of their Scarlet Beauty chambers."

She stared at him. Looked to the water. Looked at the dead woman's face at her feet.

The same low voice: "I am a sword-hand. The feupol was a gift from my brother, but I have no other arts as you in the cities do. I don't know any way I can guarantee a fast death. I have no poisons, no pretty needles."

"The darts you took from me. I can tell you where to place the tip of one, at the back of my neck, and press with a fast and steady hand. Done correctly, you will take my life instantly, painlessly."

She shook her head, frowning. "This is a fool's bargain."

"Doubt all you want. But as I have already said: you have literally nothing to risk. The m'agique will force me to confirm the name's truth the moment I lay eyes upon it. And whether it is the true prize or not, it is up to your honor whether or not you fulfill your part of the deal once it is consummated. I have no means to stop you."

She stared at the body. Chewed on her lower lip. The left edge of that nasty scar on her jawline seemed to thicken as she tightened her jaw.

A slight push. A tug. Work the knot of her doubt carefully. Her mind was a funnel, where things mostly were dropped in and eventually found some center. But a funnel was a cone downwards, a tornado that never spat up anything new or released anything of its own. Fine. A funnel's weakest place was where it touched down, where its mouth fed out the whole bottlenecked pour. Block it up, pull it apart, and a funnel was nothing.

Her mind was made with a shrug. "You're right on that much. You can't do anything looking at paper."

Pon-Chai nodded. "And if the paper is false...if the woman was wrong, or somehow all this has been for naught...you still have time to find some other place to go. You would have some time in advance of your employer realizing what's happened."

That was the last twitch, the last tug to undo the funnel of her thinking.

She rummaged into the inside of her tunic, through stitched-in plates of leather to a pocket there. Tugged out the worn and crinkled slip of paper.

Tromping over the body to his side, she leaned down and extended her arm. "You tell me if the name is here, and I will kill you as you have asked."

His eyes found the paper, and even in the gloom the black ironwood ink against the parchment was distinct enough to make out the shapes.

He stared. Squinted.

Her hand shook slightly with impatience. "Well? Is it the name or isn't it?"

His eyes were able to focus.

He saw what was written on the paper.

His face stilled.

"It's...difficult..."

"What?"

Pon-Chai rolled forward a bit more, to draw his head an inch closer to the paper.

"It's difficult...to have to pretend stupidity for so long in front of one who is the genuine article."

His freed left hand swung around from his back and slapped her wrist, hard enough to send the paper fluttering out of her hand. An ill-timed draft from the trees caught it, and sent it floating onto the water of the pond.

As she was opening her mouth to screech—at his freeing himself from her clumsy funnel-wrap knotting of his wrists or the name falling to the water—he doubled himself over, brought up both his feet, and slammed both shod limbs into her stomach. This time he got the effect he'd hoped for with his badly-chosen single-foot swipe before, and she was truly shoved back and over while he recovered his feet. Everything was hot breaths and scratching noises in the sandy earth as he put distance between them, his back nearly to the treeline.

But the shortsword swing he was expecting didn't come. Seeing the paper in the water, the woman seemed to utterly forget Pon-Chai and instead leapt into the water, making a splash that was gunpowder-loud in the still of the woods around them.

She thrashed in the water. Arms and legs spraying out fans of the fluid like diamond-glitter into the air overhead. The cricket that had earlier gone silent seemed to think this was a request for play, and began performing in the background.

Gawping, gasping, every attempt at a scream immediately glugging and galumphing on a mouthful of water.

Pon-Chai stood at the edge of the water and watched.

Why couldn't she feel out for the shallows back to safety? Oh...he could see the truth of it immediately. Just as there were no water-grasses growing the first few feet of the water.

A sinkhole pond. Where some salt dome or underground limestone cavern had collapsed and left a sizable indentation in the ground. And the groundwater of some violated aquifer had steadily bled into the hole, accumulating with infusions of rainwater to make this pond. The work of centuries, perhaps, to make this grotto. But it was deep for all its small diameter, virtually nothing but sharp drop-off once one stepped off dry land and into the waters.

The woman had leapt in after the paper...but some combination of lack of skill to swim or the heavy weight of her hidden armor plate was inevitably tiring and bearing her down.

There was never a moment, in the stretched minutes it took before her thrashing succumbed to the water and sank out of view, when he considered going for the discarded rope and offering any salvation. Pon-Chai watched her go down into the depths without moving.

When all was done, he saw the paper floating atop the water, bobbing in the dying ripples of her resistance. It had found its way to the other side of the pond. He took the time to work his way around the trees and deadfall to that side and carefully fished it out with a long stick.

The paper crumpled into pulp in his fingers. Some of the dark ink bled from the pulp like he'd crushed a worm.

Untaught didn't mean lacking for cleverness. But clearly the success of his lie proved the woman had lacked for knowledge of the finer points of the m'agique of a virtuous name. The name only had power over those it applied to. It was merely words on paper until someone invoked them.

The only thing that one knew for certain when their eyes fixed upon it was their death. And that binding rarely did anyone any good.

He rubbed his fingers together, grinding the paper to nothing before throwing it back into the water.

She died for it. Let her have it back.

"Thank you for the use of your horse," he said to the pond's again-still surface. "I consider that a more fair trade."

*

He saw no reason not to use the preparations made, and left the midwife's corpse in the pond to join her tormentor. If there was anything to any idea of a punitive and fitting hereafter, the two could be each other's hellish companions for eternity as the mineral depths held their bodies.

He left the man's body on the ground where his partner had left it in the cabin, so as not to spook the horse until it would have been time to wrap and load him up for carrying home. He gave the same low whistle to the horse as he approached it, and more pats to its neck, reaching up to rub a velvety ear, soothed the animal sufficiently for him to mount it.

The horse would shorten the travel considerably, at least back to the detour, and then to the Ice Floe. He would be able to hire a ferry or fisherboat to take him a length of the river to where the port town of Looking Glass Cloud was available, well before the Reipan district. From there, he could make the necessary arrangements for further travel.

He already knew there would be no point in going to Reipan or anywhere closer to the Annoying Isthmus. There he could only encounter some other mid-level functionary or hireling and waste more time, risk some other lucky mistake like a feupol hiding in a sleeve and waiting for his head.

The Steady is dead. The Ladder is drowned.

But have I caught the Thinker with his feet still on the rungs?

The Gheru district was at least more familiar territory for him, being the neighbor to the suburb lands where his estate lay. He already had sufficient contacts and knew the living levers to pull in order to make certain motions take place. The meeting with Third Minister was arranged, the time set. It was to be in the same coffeehouse as their first meeting.

Pon-Chai almost wanted to transmit a word to the minister about the foolishness of finishing their business in the same place where it had begun. 'The easiest way to catch a bird is in its nest,' after all. But he kept still on the matter and waited the day at a friendly home until the night of the appointed gathering. It was necessary anyway, to use the wait productively. He acquired a small scroll of clean paper, ink and a cheap set of three horsehair writing brushes.

It took a little while—and some meditation spent in his three-points position to recollect what he needed—but he was well completed and the ink dried, the papers folded, by the time he had to leave the house.

*

"You seem out of breath. Would you care for some of this brew?" The Third Minister sat in his same seat and table, already at ease with a serving of coffee. There was even the thumbprint smear of lingering silver finish on the cream carafe same as before.

Pon-Chai took his seat and smiled, giving the deferential nod of no-but-thank-you. "It was a bit of a run for me to make certain I arrived on time. I am wakeful enough this evening to drink any coffee."

His left hand itched a little. He rested the fist on his thigh. After a few moments, the itch—and its odd sensation of tugging towards the doorframe behind him—faded.

"Very well." The minister took a long sip of his own cup. Licked his lips as he replaced the cup to its saucer. Sighed with contentment. "Had the cuckoo flown far?"

"Far enough for challenge, not higher than an arrow could fly, however."

"Did you discover who the cuckoo was? Or its true keeper?"

"Yes."

"Oh? My superiors would be most grateful for that enlightenment."

"The cuckoo was merely a cuckoo. A small and annoying bird that saw an opportunity and took it. Nothing of great import to be missed. But its keeper was a bigger bird. An old hawk, perhaps of Gohlman descent even." Less-than-ideal code, but the suggestion of another bordering Empire being complicit was fine. Third Minister grimaced.

"Bothersome people, those pale savages." He poured fresh coffee into his cup. "I wasn't even aware that most people in the Gohlman could read their own tongue, let along the refinements of our dialects." A slight shake to the pouring of the coffee, and the weakest rattle of the cup bottom against the saucer before he lifted it free to sip it. His eyes wouldn't leave Pon-Chai. "Ah, but we'll pass that knowledge on to my superiors and I'm sure better...mmm... falconers than you or I can see to those fowl." The cup returned to the saucer and the minister folded his arms, the faded turquoise of his robes like a curtain of summer sky closing at his breast. "But...did you recover the egg?"

In response, Pon-Chai put out a hand and slowly opened its fingers. He withdrew the hand immediately, revealing a small twist of paper on the table, in the clear space between the coffee pot and the cream carafe.

The minister gave another of his theatrical glances about the room, though they were in the second floor private reception chamber. Pon-Chai had heard the footfalls of the attendant who had led him upstairs. They were otherwise alone up here.

Then the minister shot a hand forward, plump fingers snatching up the twist of paper and unworking the kinks and curl of it.

"What is this?" His face was a flushed salmon. His pepper-and-salt eyebrows knit together in angry puzzlement. He tossed the paper to the table.

Pon-Chai, unbothered, reached over and picked the paper up. He looked at as if needing to check its contents.

"Well...I believe it says 'TRAITOR.'" He gave a good-natured frown of insincere concern, looking up as he dropped the paper to the table. "An odd name for the Heir Emperor, I would agree."

"Where is the true name?" the minister demanded.

"At the bottom of a pond, in a lonely wood in the middle of nowhere. Along with the fools you hired to steal it and bring it to you."

"I did no such thing." A shakier hand picked up the cup and took another sip. Swallowed. Caught it badly, coughed, pounded his chest. Nearly dropped the cup returning it to the saucer. The hand went to the small steel bell beside him. "I need a fresh pot—"

"Don't worry about calling your men."

The minister's hand froze above the bell. "Excuse me?"

"The men you arranged to come in and kill me. The two who were in the empty shops on each side of here. And the one who killed and replaced the coffeehouse attendant who let me in."

"I realize that someone in your profession has to enjoy a certain amount of healthy paranoia, but—"

"They're dead, so you have no doubt of what I'm talking about." Pon-Chai glanced up at the overhead cedar beams a moment. Looking briefly for any suspicious shadows that shouldn't be there. The ceiling was clean.

"How...how could you have killed them?" The minister had forgotten to try and hide his knowledge of these things. "You couldn't bring weapons here. The sigils..."

"The sigils prevent me from bringing any of my weapons into the room, that is true." His left fist felt another sleepy twitch from the door. "But I made certain to use my weapons on those outside before I came in. Your men are holding them for me until I reclaim them. Wherever they happened to fall."

The minister recovered some of his decorum. "Y-yes...most unfortunate. I had thought our meeting might need additional s-security. I should have notified you in advance...I suppose their families will need compensation."

Pon-Chai seemed not to have heard. "I noticed two of them wore that provincial leather-plate clothing that your other mercenaries did. Do you hire them all from the same district?" He remembered the rough way of talking, the clothing, the almost defiant pride of being Untaught versus learned. "They're from the Annoying Isthmus, aren't they? Or one of the Reipan district villages near the foothills? It would make sense, hiring them from the dropoff destination. And perhaps you even got them a bit cheap, if they thought they were doing something to bring down the Empire. Did you sell them on some tale of revolution and glorious defiance of the court?"

"When I hired you, my spies had reported you were not such a conniver. I had been led to believe you were an hononrable—"

"I have the name."

The minister's mouth pursed shut. His eyes flicked to the bell but he'd withdrawn his hand. He went back to folding them against his chest, no doubt a default position when he didn't know what else to do.

"Would I presume you'd be open to a bargain? To preserve some measure of worth from this contract? I could make it quite lucrative for you—"

"The writing was destroyed, Third Minister. With no copies made. I mean to say that I have the name." He reached up and tapped a finger to his temple. "Here."

The minister's eyes narrowed. "What do you want?"

"From you? Nothing." He rose from his seat, keeping his back to the door as he gracefully stepped around his chair and pushed it in. "The advance you gave has already been transferred through the available secondaries and secured. And as for the other half of the payment...I'll consider it a necessary sacrifice for some peace of mind."

"You can't...you can't just leave here."

"Yes I can. Unless you're hiding more mercenaries in your sleeves to stop me."

His left hand was itching again, irritably so but he fought the urge to rub it against his pants to try and scratch and relieve it some. He turned and had his hand to the doorhandle when the odd rub-grind cry of chair legs pushing back, and the harsh snap-click after it, stopped him.

He turned to see the minister holding a small brass tube, with what looked like a small, reversed brass antler mounted to the sides of it near the minister's hand. The tube curved downwards into a wooden handle he held it by. The tube was only about as large around as a pencil, but the bore wasn't the threat.

Of course gunpowder was common enough. And there were weapons inspired by older times still available. Blunderbusses, muskets, rifles, single-shot so-called 'madame's friends.' Most were too expensive, troublesome, or outlawed in some districts for many to have one, but they were not unfamiliar to a man who had carefully considered the many flavors of weaponry to carry in his work, including the explosive kind.

But this was a specialized weapon, an 'Asp of Evening' gun. Using a low but focused powder load to fire not a bullet or ball but a steel pellet, hollow with a small hole bored into it. The pellet would be filled with a fast-release poison so it wouldn't matter where the minister's shaky aim got him. He would be dead in a gasping, suffocating handful of minutes.

The snap-click had been the minister cocking the little antler which was the firing pin.

"I suppose your sleeves are for more than wiping your mouth on," Pon-Chai remarked. "How did you manage to get such a delicate device past your guardian glyphs?" He tilted his head towards the doorframe behind him where the guardian glyphs still glittered in the wood carvings.

"You thought yourself clever in circumventing them your way. Mine is more simple. I own this coffeehouse. Through any number of secondary parties and false-names. But as true owner, the glyphs make exception for me alone."

Pon-Chai nodded. "Propriety. Ownership. M'agique is said to be the noble chaos, yet even it seems to bow to a certain order of formalities, doesn't it? Even out here in these 'lesser districts.'"

"Tell me the name if you expect to leave here alive."

Pon-Chai sighed and raised his other hand. The one he'd kept closed until now. He brought it to waist height.

He opened it, palm towards the minister, fingers splayed. The minister could easily see even several feet away the writing carefully inscribed on his fingers. A line went from fingertip to palm on each finger. And on his palm, along the life line, was another inscription in a tidy but dark calligraphic writing.

"You never had the power to threaten me, Third Minister. Guardian glyphs or not." He tilted his hand to show the ink more clearing in the overhead candelabra light. "Do you see these names? You will have them all before I leave."

He closed his fist. And brought it up an inch.

A sound—like a hard gale blowing through holed metal cans of ringing brass—blew through the room. The minister jerked his eyes up to the ceiling. The candelabra swung on its heavy iron chain, rattling like bells on a wire.

Pon-Chai's other hand, lowered to his side at the minister's threat, snapped forward. An underhand toss.

The minister screeched as the dart struck his hand, causing him to jerk and release the gun. Blood pattered down onto the tablecloth, turning the snowy linen into an autumn crimson. The minister shook his hand, the dart pinned into the meat of his palm. His wide eyes went to Pon-Chai almost as if he were asking him to take back his weapon, as if that would take away the wound with it. In the swinging light, the shadows of the coffee set and table legs woozed drunkenly back and forth about them. It gave the disorienting feeling of standing in the middle of some vast spinning plate.

"You bastard!" The minister's other hand was gripping his injured hand at the wrist. Wringing it, causing more blood to pool in the creases of the hand and then fall, fat and dark, to the tabletop.

"Perhaps. But not because of any infraction to you, bureaucrat. Was your career really so ungratifying that you decided to try and enrich yourself at the possible cost of the whole Empire? Was an unborn babe's station in life really such a threat to yours?"

"What trick of yours was that?" The minister snatched up a napkin and was trying inexpertly to wrap it around the wounded hand. "Some stunt with a whistle concealed outside? A partner hiding behind the door?"

"Not a trick, good sir. A spirit. A summoning. You only heard the first crack of hell's doors." He shook his closed fist lightly. "The higher I raise my hand, the wider those doors will yawn. And the four souls whose names I hold in my hand will follow the command I have clasped them to, within my palm. Your sigils were fashioned to guard against weapons of the hand. Knives, swords...but not simple ink and words."

"What...what are you talking about?"

Pon-Chai's voice was that same deadly conversationally soft tone as it had been when falsely bargaining for his own quick death in the dark woods.

"Do you know why the Emperor and his best spavinomancers, his wisest generals and war advisers, have never in all the centuries of rule, used magic to raise the dead to fight for them? Are you privy to that much worldly knowledge, Third Minister Willow-Adjunct?"

"What?"

"Because as tempting as that power is...and believe me, they have that power...the dead ultimately know no true master on earth. No living being can command the dead to fight for them." He took a slow breath. "The dead are not soldiers or spies, not archers or infantry. The dead are merely the agonized. They are the screaming and the furious. It is easier to command a wind to sink a sailing ship and hope it blows off to the horizon, than to call up a single soul and pray that when it does what you have ordered it that it doesn't simply turn about and find your eyes and tongue a fitting payment for its labor."

"This is a trick!"

Pon-Chai shook his head, almost sounding regretful. "The dead are no trick. Four souls. Merely four names that I knew from past affairs. And those four inscribed in the right formation to call them tonight, here. For you."

He shook the fist gently, and there was the distant sound of glass and crockery smashing downstairs, as if someone had gotten drunkenly angry with the coffee's quality. Someone hollering at the sudden activity. Someone's sandaled feet clodded on the first step towards the upper room.

Pon-Chai raised the fist an inch, just an inch.

From downstairs came a scream and no more footfalls on the staircase. The ululating, ragged cry sounded as though it was being exploded to the limit of a human throat short of rupturing. Then cut off.

"That would be the attendant. Your last mercenary." He tilted his head a little. "Their first victim."

"Nothing...you have nothing like...this isn't..." The minister was bewildered. The napkin was soaked halfway through with dark red. A fresh drop found its way through the linen to the floor, and the floorboards began to rattle under their feet. Dust shivered down from the beams overhead.

"Careful with that hand," Pon-Chai cautioned. "They home on blood more than anything else. It...enrages them. I suppose as much as a man dying of thirst arriving at a cool fountain, only to find it saltwater."

"This is a ridiculous trick!"

"Your files on me should have been more thorough," Pon-Chai said quietly. "Perhaps your spies should have been paid a little more to take the trouble." He raised his fist another inch. and the floorboards rattled an octave harder, as if someone were firing rifle rounds rapidly underneath them.

The candelabra overhead swung so hard the chain snapped, sending it crashing into a corner of the room.

Third Minister's glance whirled around him, taking in the floorboards and then solidifying on Pon-Chai's fist. "You are no wielder of m'agique! Everyone knows—"

"Do they know?" Pon-Chai finally allowed a thin smile. "Do they know everything about me, as they know my virtuous name?" He tilted his head as if to look at the Third Minister like a dog hearing an odd sound. "What of you, Third Minister? What does everyone know about you?"

The floorboards clattered hard enough that the tables in the room resting atop them rattled as well. A coffee cup fell to the floor from the edge of the

Third Minister's and shattered with a brittle bell sound.

"You were very foolish while trying to be so clever, Third Minister." Pon-Chai's fist stayed in place as if made of hardened clay into a brick form. "You outwitted yourself."

"I don't—"

"You paid your spies poorly and took their reports as the gospel of me. Of my abilities, my parentage."

"A poor populist writer and a spoiled merchant's daughter is hardly a parentage," the minister spat.

Pon-Chai refused the bait and remained calm.

"You tried to have me killed upon confirmation that I had accomplished my task. You tried to mask it as some sort of act of the greater state, a necessary sacrifice of a well-reputed resource in the name of the Heir Emperor's safety...when in reality it was to cover your tracks and make sure no one but you would ultimately have the Heir's name."

"A filthy lie."

"No. Worse. A filthy truth. Your assignment did not make sense for a sensitive matter of state. Find the thief, kill him, bring back the name? A real minister seeking to quietly protect the Heir would have had me kill the thief, yes...perhaps even have me killed in case I tried to double-cross you for greater profit." Pon-Chai lowered his fist back to its starting position, and the floorboards settled to a low shiver of wood clacks. "But bring back the name? The virtuous name of the Heir Emperor? No. Only a pathetic Third Minister seeking to rapidly increase his power and station from his glue-stuck, backwoods assignation in the Gheru district would ask that of a professional like me."

Downstairs, a horrific scrabbling noise had begun. As if someone had unstopped a box filled with untold hordes of rats and sent them off in a starved frenzy across every floorboard in the chamber below. But the sandy-scrape noises were so heavy. Rats and other things from dark spaces.

The minister's eyes rolled down to the floor at his feet, back to Pon-Chai. He licked his lips.

"I had to make sure the name was truly destroyed."

Pon-Chai shook his head. "No. If you couldn't trust that I would do my job, why hire me at all? You knew my reputation in the first place. And if you weren't sure of how I would complete the task, you would have had me destroy the writing, then have me killed. You had the woman escorted by Untaught hirelings. Killers who specifically could not read any writing so would bring you the name without a risk they'd read it for themselves. You hired me as a smokescreen. You assumed that waiting a few days...the days that you had to wait anyway until the Stork could get your pigeon out of the capital...would be sufficient that anyone hired to recover the name would fail, and you would have a simple way of going to anyone who might question you and showing evidence of your loyalty, your earnest attempt to help. You are low enough on the greater tiers of the Empire's offices that you perhaps would get a mild reprimand yet keep your head. There are much bigger names than yours to be executed soon for this failure of security anyway. But your killers were very specific before they died."

Third Minister's face betrayed a faint wince, just a pinch of the eyes for a second. Did he think any of his men would have been spared even now? Was it really such a surprise to hear they were dead? A drop of his blood hit the floor, and the scrabbling down below increased briefly. There was the sound like heavy brass fingers tapping, feeling at the bottom steps of the staircase.

"They fought the hardest to make sure the name was not destroyed or lost. One of them even drowned for it. That was all the proof I needed of who was truly responsible...you arranged to take the Heir's name. You...maybe the first person ever, though there are few new stories under the sun...saw a weakness in the system and moved to exploit it. But you went cheap. Like all mid-level bureaucrats, for your first attempt you tried to go cheap as you thought you could afford."

"Clearly, all of you in your profession are overpriced." But Third Minister barely had any venom in his voice. Another drop of blood fell to the floor and the floorboard it land on began to lightly smoke, as if a fire had started downstairs.

"Perhaps. You probably even tried to haggle with the mercenaries. I'm sure you didn't even bother to have the midwife haggled, she was probably grateful for any money. Or perhaps you had some leverage on her to force the issue? It doesn't matter. And perhaps you didn't even seek it to wield its power for yourself. Why not head east and see if perhaps one of the Pashmir warlords would give a small kingdom for such a treasure? Or perhaps even go as far as the Gohlman Empire and their Emperor?"

"No doubt you thought of such things yourself."

"Surprisingly, no." Pon-Chai shook his head. "I like where I live. I know the people. I know the language, the food, the coffee. Unlike you, I am happy where I am, even with its difficulties."

"Then it occurred to you to keep it for yourself. Perhaps wield power yourself over the dynasty? A pathetic killer turned royalty with but a word?"

Pon-Chai betrayed nothing, but his fist rose again and let the floorboards resume their louder din.

The minister screamed. "Stop this!"

"I have no power to stop any of this now. You have done your dance on the ladder, Third Minister, and you finally jumped down hard one time too many. The Ladder is broken. The steady hand securing it below for you is gone. You are the only one left. And you set your own death in motion the moment you hired me."

"Maybe it's your death that is now impending," the Third Minister leered, trying to rally a petty courage. "Perhaps my contingency in the event that you were truly successful and returned here...was your virtuous name. In my hands." He beamed a savage smile even as his wounded hand was shaking harder. More smoke rose from other drops of blood on the floor.

Pon-Chai looked at him, stunned. The Third Minister's smile grew another several degrees wider in its arc.

Then Pon-Chai's astonishment transmuted to a snap of high, balanced laughing.

"Don't mock me!" The minister snarled, sweat collecting down his cheeks. "I can end you at any moment, but you are still capable of walking—"

"Oh shut up." Pon-Chai spat back at him, all momentary humor evaporated. "You could not have my name if you bribed all the Record General offices in the world at once. I secured the archive of my name when I started my profession and destroyed it. You cannot bargain with what you don't have, and you cannot have what I have secured against all thievery."

Third Minister dropped his cat's smile.

"No one can break into the Recorder General offices or their archives."

"And no one can steal a royal name right out of the Imperial palace. And the thiefkiller doesn't use *magique*. The world is full of things that are impossible."

Now at last the minister dropped all pretense at supremacy. "Please—"

"No." Pon-Chai reached his free hand behind him, on the doorhandle. "Even if I wanted to, I want to live more. To call forth the dead, one's only hope for walking away is to give them something else to vent their rage upon. Someone else." The minister's mouth gawped open, a drying tongue like a pinkish-gray slug that lay useless at last. "You should have left it all alone, Third Minister. You should have truly listened, not just recited, the old poetry."

Third Minister's face paled to the color of rain faded birch wood, silvered and bloodless. *"Leave the living to be raised—"*

"—leave the dead to rise," Pon-Chai finished, nodding, and jerked his fist up to head height as his other hand tugged open the door, his body with that eerie grace stepping to the side as it opened.

From downstairs came a roar that seemed to pour out of a thousand lion's throats. Several of the floorboards were smoking hard enough to make a haze in the room. The scrabble-scratching turned instead into the kind of whipsawing growl-grown of desert sandstorms, spitting static lightning and scalding sands, as you might encounter in the far western provinces.

And into the room, barreling through the opened door...something that was pale gray as bones covered in the ash of pyres. A smoke and cinders cloud made of shattered porcelain, fork tines bent off from their cutlery. Teeth, still yellowed as ivory and wet. There was underneath it all the queer patter like a spring rainstorm breaking atop a tin roof. Drumming and drumming.

Pon-Chai lowered his head, turning around and leaving by the door as swiftly but unobtrusively as he could behind the tail of the flying shapes. Everything was the din of screams, the whirl of shattered crockery, shredding linen, metal coffeeware spanging and tolling off from the walls, denting and crushing with the ease of a circus strongman boot-stomping it on a stone stair. It seemed impossible for one person to be noticed amidst it.

He held his hand high as he took the stairs. He didn't look at any of the destruction on the ground floor, keeping his eyes on the ends of his shoes to navigate the wreckage-strewn floor. When he saw a finger, he didn't change pace but simply pushed it aside with the toe of his shoe and exited.

Upstairs, the whirlwind was now a dark red. And the shredding sounds amongst the gibbering and breathless, endless screaming was richer. Wetter.

The screaming winds cried out sins, names, promises to carry anyone in its reach away to places that didn't even have social names, they were too feared in the afterlife to want to even invoke in thought. They did their work fast.

But that was not to say they did not take every opportunity to savor this time out in the living air.

*

Pon-Chai walked away from the coffeehouse as the roaring, snarling sounds quickly turned into helpless, defeated wails. One or two meats was not enough to make the risen dead happy in their furor. They turned their teeth and nails to the very walls and floor of the building. Armed now with jagged rips of metal, bits of bone as spearheads, the spirits were paying tribute to their own agonies by marking everything around them with the imprint of their self-loathing.

He refused to look back, finally opening his fist and lowering it as he fell into a fast walk.

Looking back was one of the weakest and easiest ways that fools who invoked the departed could become their next meal. The eyes are the windows to the soul, his father had remarked once, but quickly made sure to note it was no line of his. And the freed souls could find a window opened in a glance, an ill-timed look out of curiosity. A window opened that they could climb through quite speedily.

A ladder down from a window is as easily a ladder up to one.

Should have paid your spies better. Should have taken more care in reading your reports and files about me. To know that I did not follow in the training of my parents despite all their money and hopes that I would do so.

Should have seen that my father was the writer.

But my mother was the witch.

To invoke the names of the dead was not a small thing. But his mother had been skilled in whispering a name to the sky and having only a single cloud she wanted hear its beckoning. He had never taken her practice, but he had watched and learned her skills before leaving home.

And when he had come home for the funeral, and seen his mother, inscribing the flesh of her breast over her heart with his father's true name. When he had seen her nearly in griefstricken haste do what he had just done with deliberate malice to the minister. That was when he had decided she must come live with him. Keep her from feeling the need to bring the dead back as pale proxy for the compassionate living.

There was an alarm being raised in the nearby darkened establishments as the riot of noise and destruction of the coffeehouse—and the remains of the Third Minister inside them—became common knowledge. Someone was yelling 'fire,' another was yelling 'raid.'

No need for more on your soul than you already have. He stopped to close his eyes and whisper the conjure-names that had brought forth the dead. In reversal-words, with the *m'agique* whistling from him and out into the night. The last measure was to blow across his spread hand, the draft of his breath carrying out the last of the energy to disperse them.

The clattering and wailing ceased instantly, as if a hand had clapped down on a table and slapped the silence into place. The last terrible sound was the deep, vibrating groan and thunderclap. As of a great door closing. All that remained were the noises of the remains of the coffeehouse collapsing in on itself, and the cries of latecomers coming out to see what was the matter.

He looked at his hand. The writing had disappeared.

Pon-Chai used the cover of the noises to leave the district and get back to his briefly rented rooms, to sleep and gather energy for the trip home.

It was quiet in his home. A day's travel even using a merchant's cart to hop a brief ride, returning from Gheru district and stopping off to clean and change his things at his way station in Twining Ivy Traps.

The house was all the more seemingly silent compared to all the city noise he'd grown accustomed as background in his ears throughout the contract.

When he came in the front door, he did not call out. It was late evening, almost full dark outside, and his mother would be napping in her chair by the fire in the reading room.

He went to the kitchen, leaving the small satchel he'd purchased along the trip on the preparing table there. The ice chest was still fairly fresh, and he drank two cups of cold milk and sliced the heel off a half-finished but still fresh loaf of brown bread in the breadbox.

There were people who considered themselves well-traveled that he had spoken to before. Many of them said the same things, most notably that you appreciated home more every time you returned to it from a long trek...and that somehow travel made the world smaller and larger at the same time. Like an optic trick of glass and light in a magic lanternist's performance.

The first was true every time. But the second...Pon-Chai chewed the bread slowly and swallowed, considering that rarely did the world feel smaller when he came home. He put a cup of water inside the oven and struck up the gaslight to heat it. Stood with his back against the counter, arms folded, eyes cast to the tabletop while the water warmed.

Every time he returned alive from a contract...every time he came back from one of his disappeared places from the old maps...the world felt so much larger. All one had to do was open up the Imperial Roads & Ways, any five-year edition, and see where the maps trailed off into places beyond what any cartomancer could chart with their *màgique* and tracking charms and placement chants. That told you plenty about the real size of the world.

More than that, though, he thought that what he really felt after every journey was that the world was...thicker? Deeper. Yes. Deep. Steeped in time. So many cultures and Empires and civilizations that pre-dated the great intercommunications, before the multiple near-Falls and Revolutions and Revisions, all coming into life and growing and reaching, touching like the fingertips of blind boxers trying to discover their opponents before hesitantly throwing the first sightless blows. And others finding each other like the roots of different but elderly trees...the roots finding each other and cracking through stone and soil to intertwine, to begin to feed a now-shared life across the meadows, under the ground of centuries and millennia.

The world did not get smaller with every trip. It only grew deeper. Older. Richer. The atlases...just got more inadequate.

*

He finished the bread and sighed. Outside, crickets were beginning to truly play their concertos and reed flutes in earnest as he walked to the reading room, the cup in one hand and his other hand slowly lowering the sachet of lemon and mint tea into the fluid.

She was sitting next to a nearly-dead fire, her blankets bunched in the lap and about the shoulders as ever. Her iron hair, still thick and lustrous, shone in the hall's lamplight as he came in. He sat the cup on the small lacquer table next to her chair, then hunched down at the hearth to freshen the flame and add a log to it. Her eyes were closed, her hands each resting on a thigh like two white river stones, soft and round in the weak light.

Only with a fresh tongue of flame licking up the fireplace's stone wall and seated in his own chair did he give a long breath. Feel his toes un-tighten inside his shoes. Feel his back soften to the cushions underneath him.

"Mother? I brought you tea. It's on the table." He picked up a small folio of drawings he'd started to leaf through when the last crimson note had been delivered and interrupted things. The fine-lined inkings, delicately washed in colors as if the tints and tones had fluttered as petals of light to settle on each page just where they were needed, but only that and barely adding any weight to the paper of the page. Depictions of cities that disappeared into faint blue-lined clouds...an elephant with a village on its back, traveling through a dense jungle. Fairy-tale images, but the book's publishers had included no text to indicate if these were drawings of fantasy or of real places. It was the book's simple title, *Drawings of the Granted Lands*, that had got him to look through it and purchase it to begin with.

He was absorbed in the drawings almost an hour before the silence alerted him. He put the book of drawings down to move forward, out of his seat and closer to her, looking up into her face under the still-lustrous hair.

Her tea was cold. And so was she.

He straightened her blankets. When they were neatened, his roving hands finally could not find any other place but to stop and come to rest, left on top of right, on one of her covered knees as he stared at her.

"Thank you, Mother."

He swallowed deeply. Once. Twice. Hard.

"Thank you for my name."

You were named for a great poet, the greatest poet of all the times. What will you make of that name, that destiny despoiled?

"Thank you for the *m'agique*...not that rose with the dead, but for that simple spell of love that never broke. Please tell my father it was not disdain for his works that drove me, but shame for my own. And that I hope you both find forgiveness in your new hearts."

He picked up her tea and took it back to the kitchen to empty it and wash it out in the sink. The entire series of movements were mechanical, without thought, like much of his life as a thiefkiller.

With the last click of the porcelain as he left the cup on the counter to finish drying, he stared at his new satchel on the preparation table.

He took a breath.

He took another.

A few preparations. A few last necessary things. A handful of the required formalities. Two days? Four. It will be four. No more.

But before those could be started, before another frame could be righted or a blanket folded, this last.

He stepped out to the rear porch. He looked out at the night sky. He heard the crickets serenading the velvet clouds, and somewhere in the far hedge there was something digging...a rabbit or possum, seeking a tasty root to fill its belly another night.

He opened his mouth, and from his throat issued the quietest, almost non-voice. Barely the hush of a curtain drawn in an empty parlor.

His mother's virtuous name, to be uttered at the end by the only one she'd trusted with it when her husband was gone. Her true name, spoken to the night's sky that it would carry it up and eventually be remarried to her somewhere in the hereafter.

And with that, the last of what was entrusted to him as he'd promised to that years-gone father. The last promise made as a sop to try and get the man's forgiveness before his passing. The last promise fulfilled.

A few days, yes, a few days and no more to complete the rest and see to rights.

The ginger hair had darkened the last few years, but otherwise the girl was still not yet experienced enough to yet be able to read the wrinkles in the peppers to tell which were ripe and ready and dried for making the Winter's Chill soup.

He must have changed more than he'd thought in that same time, or it was simply outright shock at his appearance at all in the village. It took her a solid few breaths of staring at his unblinking eyes to make the recognition.

"Aspic?"

"Hello, Bandy."

The two stared, smiling wider with each heartbeat, until finally something caught in his throat and she coughed. He chuckled.

"I know a good soup recipe that might help with that," he said dryly.

"Are you visiting again?"

"Yes and no."

She frowned. "How is that?"

"I'm visiting, yes. But..." he looked over his shoulder, up at the mountain range in the distance, erased in places with swatches of silver cloud. "...but I don't think I'll be leaving." He looked back at her, suddenly shy and nervous as a schoolboy before his teacher caught in whispering between desks. "If...

you would like me to."

"I would like that, yes."

Another long silence. This one far less uncomfortable or nervous.

"If you're really staying...can you tell me...?"

The old rules applied, in country or in city.

Only your parents and your greatest betrothed should ever have your virtuous name. They may have it, and the Recorder General who bestowed it to you. Your name was not cheaply had, child. It should not be cheapened by you giving it away to whomever asks...

Very gently, very slowly, he approached her.

He put his satchel—now quite roadworn and dusty and no longer new—on the floor.

You are only as vulnerable as you let yourself be. Your name and who you give it to are only as great a danger as you given them the capabilities to be.

All around them were the firecracker strings of dried peppers in the drying shed, with the sunlight a cool metallic blue outside. And cider-tree blossoms all about the ground, some of them blowing on a faint draft into the open doorway and between their feet.

He did all of this without breaking eye contact.

Her kiss was as sharp with the lingering taste of dried pepper and spices. And warmed greater than any soup or home fire he had ever had.

Then his lips moved to her ear, and whispered with a puff of summer breeze and mint.

"I am Pon-Chai, after the Great Poet of the 47th Dynasty, in the Caillou district."

Between them, something stirred the blossoms and the peppers, setting them flickering and swinging gently. She sucked in a weak breath to hear him speak, and felt the *m'agique* of that moment pass from his heart to hers.

Will this place stay off the maps? He considered the fragility of such lost places and their serenity. But then he remembered a rather smiling shadow of a reality that was now available to him, uniquely apart from anyone else in the Empire.

If the Emperor and his armies ever do *turn their eyes this way...well, I have a* name *I could drop to stop that.*

He leaned back, smiling.

She started to lean forward, to bring her mouth to his ear, but he stopped her by taking her shoulders in his hands, soft and as pine boughs caressing the barest skin of a pond underneath their outstretched branches. The water ripples shivered through her.

"Not now," he told her. "For now you are Bandy and this is a place called Peaceful. And I don't care what the virtuous record of you is called. I only know that I call you Loved, and by none in the world so much as me."

Her next kiss was more familiar in its taste. But no less wonderful for the repetition of its verse. And it confirmed what he had known for most of his life: he was no poet or writer, to try and put any of her into words.

"Real poetry, is to lead a beautiful life. To live poetry is better than to write it."
—Matsuo Bashō

Ron Horsley is an artist/writer living in Columbus, Ohio.

He is the author of the "Everything Under" novels featuring the urban fantasy adventures of Body & Soul. He is also the author of "The World" series of illustrated children's novels and stories starting with the critically-acclaimed *Beyond the Grass Ocean*. He is an MFA Graduate of the Columbus College of Art and Design as well as a 2002 Alumnus of the Clarion Workshop for Fantasy & SciFi Writing.

For blog updates, portfolio works and news about upcoming projects and new writing, check out **RonHorsley.com**

To find out about "The World" series of children's novels, visit **BeyondTheGrassOcean.com**

For more about the "Everything Under" novels, visit **Everything-Under.net**

www.ingramcontent.com/pod-product-compliance
Lightning Source LLC
Chambersburg PA
CBHW052007170626
46808CB00007B/2809